Notes to Self

www.theronniles.com

TAI SMITH

My Son, no matter what, you're my messenger.

I will always Love You Dearly.

Forever and Ever, until the end of my time

DIRECTION OF THERON'S STORYLINE

Story1. The Cracked Ladder

Reality Check 1

Story 2.Rediscovering Music

Story 3. For The Love of Bojangles

Story 4. A Return to Reality

Reality Check 2

Story 5. The Alternative Psychoanalysis

Story 6. Blue Legato: A Child's Religion

Story 7. A New Generation of Jive

Story 8. A Reprise of Yester-Year: Vintage Jive

Story 9. Eu Nao Estou Enfermo

Reality Check 3

AFTERTHOUGHTS

INTRODUCTION

My name is Tai L. Smith. Sometimes, that name doesn't fit me. It blankets me. Covers my real persona and mutes my luster. I had to fight to understand that a name is but a brand or more to the point, a label. And during that eternal fight with myself, and while battling the bulk of inner issues that I have walked with through life thus far, I decided to capitalize on the one action that I can do without reservation. Before you, more or less, are the components and abstract notes of that realization. I have found that the imagination, coupled with writing, can be used to access a gateway to an inner-world that we all have found or are still searching to find. Fiction, the subconscious of one's imagination, is the only possession guarded by my own rule and dictatorship and without outside intrusion. In reaching the peaks of self-discovery, you find that certain truths that you hold dear are the seeds planted and reaped into your mind by others (parents, family, and society). For a lifetime, I have lived in a paradigm of other, thus lacking the knowledge of my inner-self. The name that I have, the morals and ethics that I once believed, and the perceptions that were planted in my head, were not of my own manifestation. Though these reaped ideals have served as a solid launching pad for self-discovery.

In attempting to find out more about myself beyond physical attributes, and reprogramming my mind from the other and according to the education that I received from living, I stumbled upon this beautiful epiphany of art and craft. Thus I realized that mental freedom is the end product of self-discovery. I was a hungry mind, starving for an escape away from the rest of the world, and that longing forced me to waste no time in putting all of my creative thoughts onto paper. While working in retail to pay for the college time that I needed, my only comfort was the sound of a pen to a receipt or a pencil to a paper bag. I crept through the workday. During class time in college, I jotted down ideas. College was the first rung of many, in which I would have to climb to understand what type of individual I was. All based wholly upon the "gift" that my family imparted to me. As I learned the basic nuances of life while moving from place to place throughout America, I utilized all aspects of life experiences to gauge my personal being. While at nightclubs dancing, and at house parties, I would defy the pressures of other (peers) and would float to this world and write every single thought that I had about myself and the people that were around me. Napkins, toilet paper, beer bottle wrappers, brown paper bags, my hands, rolling papers, all became my sacred letter head, as I pieced together these thoughts. When I would get the sensation to walk in my other world, I could hear Timbale drums pounding in the background and the setting placed me against a tiger. The image in my mind was of me, and I delicately signed my name onto my finished work. In retrospect, the name, Theron Niles, serves as a direct connection between the realization of life, and the expectations that one might have of one's self, between the stages of late adolescence to middle adulthood. I have laid before the reader many of man's fears, dreams, ambitions, and presented those in a fictitious form, according to the World as I have seen it.

In my mind, I metaphysically and unconsciously ran from this tiger that was as thin as I, and assumed that because it was chasing me in my world, that it was extremely hungry. I didn't know what the animals' objective was, but I felt that I would have to kill him in order to feel secure. The only problem was that I had the faintest idea on how to kill a tiger without a large gun. So in my defense, I would run and hide to avoid death, hence searching my vast continent of infinite ideas and perspectives for a gun to slay this tiger. I ran from the beast, night and day. I would stop underneath waterfalls to write. I stopped in Aboriginal villages attempting to barter for a gun, while I wrote. During the eruption of far off volcano's I would stop and write. While sleeping and hearing the pounding of timbale drums, I jotted down notes into my conscious and kept the peripheral of my imagination open just in case I would awaken to the grizzly snarl of the roaming beast. I prayed to God that a moments rest would suffice before I would see the tiger from a distance, and have to run. Even when this perfect scene in my mind was cloudy, raining, snowing or what have you, with my shoulder bag, a dicta-phone recorder, and a pen, the timbale drum's would pound in the background, and I would run to hide, hide to write, and sleep just enough to search for that gun. Finally exhausted, mentally and physically, I realized that if I hadn't found a gun after years of running, that maybe I didn't need a gun in the first place. Conventional wisdom forced me to find a conscious median point so that I would not have to run for the rest of my life, without the crutch of a weapon. It was more practical to feed the hungry beast than to assume that it only wanted me for dinner. The growing wisdom of twenty years of life, further whispered to me that I couldn't barter with other humans who clutched some sort of weapon for their physical and mental protection. This book of short stories then became a manifestation of me not slaughtering the beast, but taming the beast's rage through domestication. Until I wrote this complete experience onto paper, and shared it with others, I would run forever. Every man and woman on God's great Earth has their own scene and their own music blaring in the background. I hope this piece of art will inspire those men and women who are searching, to conquer whatever beast that they may be running from, unconsciously or otherwise.

It has been a long time coming, but I knew that some type of change would come. That change only came when I maintained composure, accepted the Grace of God, and walked across this vast land with confidence based on that higher Faith.

I feel that my mind is now unhinged for a little while, and for the time being. I am now free to roam through my conscious, my imagination and my soul without feeling like I do not know me, and that I might have to get up at any moment and run. Read the stories in this piece for fiction, and the reality checks as interludes to reality. With that seed planted in your mind, and with a strong motive to entertain those with limited patience for entertainment, I offer you, my "Notes to Self".

"Mind"

By Tai Smith

"The gateway to freedom or to prison-that which is physical, and God forbid, mental."

Story 1:

The Cracked Ladder

DAY 3

A faint glimpse of sunlight flutters through a cobweb-covered window, as Junior tries to locate where exactly his makeshift basketball court once stood. He had been through a natural war zone the days before, and since then, has been relegated to a room for a crime that neither he nor his family committed. He is but a child, but oftentimes a child in his circumstances catches it the worse. Across from him is his mother, who was weak to begin with. She doesn't eat much, and sleep much. She just works as many shifts as possible, as a concierge to make ends meet. On the other side of the ladder, is where she normally kills herself to make sure that her children get by. And after the concierge nights comes the washing of dishes and vacuuming floors, while pretending that tomorrow will be better. Lona, Junior's older sister has been missing for a couple of days now. She went camping with the girl scouts from the ritzy part of the city. She just missed the cracking of the ladder. Junior supposes that she is okay. He gazes at other things moving slowly past his home base. He reminisced, as a child does when things were much simpler and life was a little more predictable. He remembers climbing the

14

fence with his friend Piccolo during the hottest day of the summer, and grabbing one of the milk crates that no longer was being used, and that had a bottom already gone. Piccolo was Junior's best friend. They met during the first day of school when they were youngsters. Five years had passed and an eleven year old can grow as old as the environment he lives in. Junior and Piccolo would sit and throw rocks into the creek after school. The creek ran back about three yards behind Junior's house, and his daddy, Terry "Big Tone" Delacroix had strung an old tire from the rubber factory atop and down a tall branch, and roped it perfectly so that it hung about a foot above the shallow creek. This would be Junior's little sanctuary away from the hustle and bustle of the neighborhood. A simple neighborhood it was. Either work honestly, or work as the streets tell you. Either way you had to work. Just depends on what sort of work you did. What morals you want to use. Junior knew that Piccolo's life wasn't that great, but also knew that despite his mother's affliction and his father's habit, that Piccolo didn't have the outlet that he had. It was the summer after the first grade when Piccolo and Junior would learn about life. The two of them would just sit by the creek chucking rocks toward the big ladder to the sky, while watching turtles and gators swim through. Junior could feel that someone was waiting. A lot of the people of the World waited. And yet still, as he stares from the attic window, he sees the same small critters float by. Sometimes Junior and Piccolo would take turns swinging on the tire. Out over the creek, back to the side, and upon each other's turn, a hand or two-a caption- of each other's small hands would leave in and out of the picture. Even when it rained, Piccolo and Junior would sit on the side and just let the day and the heat, along with the sirens and breeze pass through. The ladder was always soothing. For, everyone always worried about the un-thinkable, never quite believing that the one-day would be like that doomsday. It would be Armageddon for a community who grew old and rusted like the ladder. Instead, the community would only concern themselves with the here and now, and Junior and Piccolo just passed time. Each day, Junior would walk Piccolo home. Their tattered shoes and shirts, their nappy skulls, would never stop to ever listen to what was whispered to them along the way. It was too scary for kids. They just followed the sky that was dimly lit from afar by the full moon, and talked about the basketball court that they were to build aside Junior's house. Piccolo's house wouldn't be a great place to build a basketball court. For one, too many people lurked on the outsides, and in the alleyway were trash and old smelly mattresses and bottomed out sofas. Syringes and broken pipes were strewn across the concrete ground as well. There was always some trouble next door to Piccolo's house, which his grandma, his momma, his six sisters, and his father, all lived in. Junior always thought that the reason Piccolo was always at his house was because of the noise, and the people and all his sisters. Sometimes, he would go home and his father would lock the door from the outside and then climb back in through the window. Not because he wanted to, but because it was safer. You never know what lurked around in the still of the night, when folks was trying to sleep. You never knew. Piccolo's father, Goodie, knew better than to think that his family was safe from the folks that lurked around the building.

Day 4

Junior awakens to the sound of absolutely nothing, which was strange for his neighborhood. But his hunger and thirst would not allow him to move another muscle. He smiled though, because the day seemed warmer, and he was mighty cold the day before. His father lies but two steps from him, and he walks over to see what he had seen for two days before; his father sleeping. His mother, Darling, was beautiful with long flowing hair, and octoroon features-her features were African yet her skin was the tone of her grandmother's owner, and she was a physical reminder of those indiscretions. She did her usual thing of curling up in the corner and rocking to the sounds of water inching by. The creek could always be heard on a quiet morning. Mornings were usually quiet before a funeral was fixing to march through. Junior adjusted his palate on the floor, and just continued his thoughts from the previous day. He and Piccolo realized that a milk crate wouldn't last long and figured that they would be better off finding a real basketball rim. Piccolo remembered that a basketball court that was torn down in the old park where rusted door Chevy's and their homeless owners, as well as the faceless people with habits lay, probably still had a rim that nobody would ever use. The two of them ran through the carcasses that grazed in the sweltering heat, chatting with the others as if hell wasn't what they walked through, and thought of

18

the moment that just passed, as if those voices knew that the boys was trying to find something to do. The homeless graveyard yielded no basketball court, so the boys kept walking. In their walk, they would laugh at the oddities and peculiar things that happen when a funeral processional goes down. They respected the family enough to wait on the sidewalk, and walk when the final horn play subsided in the distance. Finally, they found an old basketball rim, across from the graveyard, and atop an old scrap heap, just as Piccolo thought they might find something, and took turns hauling it back to the edge of Junior's neighborhood. They worked all day and nearly night trying to nail the hoop onto the side of the house, as they would alternate climbing a trash can to do so. They were forewarned by Darling to be careful not to knock the siding off because the house was old. Junior and Piccolo made sure that the hoop was nice and sturdy, and perfectly centered. Piccolo had borrowed a piece of sidewalk chalk from one of his sisters and the two gently sketched a foul line and a boundary around the court. The only thing they needed next was to find a ball to play with. That was the only thing that kept them from playing.

Day 5

Junior awakens to a couple of birds singing, as he his mouth was full of cotton, and his fragile body could move but so much. He looked over for his mother and father but they were gone. He stared out the window, wondering what will happen. He watches as people, cars, and debris float pass his house at a quickening pace. He can only think back to how close he was to finishing his basketball court. He had never been confined to one place ever, except this time. This one time, and he couldn't even control this. The ladder cracked. Everybody talked about getting away from the ladder years ago, but somehow, no one ever thought that it would happen. Junior adjusted himself, staring out the window, right down where his basketball court was. He drifted off to sleep, as Piccolo waved from the distance for him to come out and play. He was hungry and tired, and couldn't move too much, but sitting in that attic for five days with his mother and father in an endless sleep, and no help on the horizon, he had to find Piccolo and play some basketball.

Story 2:

Rediscovering Music

Monuments tumble, dust collects. A human life has changed. Many years pass, and yet still, those times seem to blink. I did not regret a thing. For one to regret growth is one who is foolish. Never really knowing that to grow, one must die. To die, one must have flourished and taken in the sun, while feeling the dews of dawn and the rains of a day's storm trickle down a protective windowpane. Four years are gone. My first and last is signed, sealed. I have never been happier. Happiness is the ever-elusive solvent to a life devoid. It is what we humans seek. Finding it on our own is for not, due to our fear. Marriage can never hide him. A relationship can never quell its hunger. Fear will force opposites together, and leave all involved stagnant.

I met her while connecting in Newark. Who would have thought that a diamond would be lying unclaimed in the lost and found? It was glimmering blue through a field of clairvoyant gray. There she was, with her deep brown doe eyes. Her mole hair ensemble allowed her breasts to sag lowly and her hips to spread freely. Eve dripped from her essence, oozing from every one of her mannerisms. Adam secretly longs while sitting from afar wondering, albeit strategizing. I only deal with professional or exotic women-she longs but can't afford to. Is she on my level financially, professionally or socially? Does she originate somewhere that was far enough for me to be adventurous? My game has been seen under the sun for eternity. By the designer clothing and large volume of perfume, I knew that she was an American. Her soft body also supported a red hat and a red scarf, as those things behind her dark shades summoned me. A matador strolled deep within me, quelling me when I got too anxious, enticing me to act in frenzy. She had shown me lust unlike any that I had pursued or dared to vibe with. Her call, it whispered to me. It was my mother's yell, muted. "Come in for dinner." Upset. Embarrassment in front of my friends would overcome me. My mother was calling my name at the top of her lungs. Whatever she cooked, I acquiesced, would humble the embarrassment and outweigh the playing. This woman was the epiphany of that dinner. Though I stood amongst many nameless faces, at attention to this red flag, there were pleasures beneath her. With a mouth full of rocks, coupled with heart pounding temptation, I transcended back into my childhood. Walking, slowly gliding to the front of the classroom. Present the science project. Except now, I am bolder, settled with horns and a fury of snot flowing from my hooked nostril, and I approached.

"Might I sit?"

An arrogant hint of anxiety overcame me. But before she could say a word, I sat. A bull never waits for the flag to be snatched away. He lunges and reaches, all the while taking a stand to unleash his emotion. Never had I come on this strong. Never had I come across a woman as breathtaking, in an airport- the Newark Airport. I never opened my eyes and my reality wide enough to look. I never took that extra glance at a life as I did at a Dali painting. Clocks probably would ooze. Dogs would walk atop long pachyderm limbs. The sun would weep cool rain. Man would be animals and serpents. I finally opened my eyes and she was the first woman that I encountered in my awakening. Ten minutes. Seconds roll past the Renaissance and all of contemporary art history and I'm merely sitting down and staring. She tried her best to ignore me. I questioned me, and whether it was appropriate and right to approach such a woman. Adam never thought twice about Eve. Romeo soon died for Juliet.

Many men lost fortune for her and the posture she maintained; back arched in a perfect S shape. I grew weary of the many eye rolls that she peered. Maybe she harvested a strong distaste for black men.

Chivalry is but a word contrived to drive men mad. The word suggests craziness. It should be dead. I would soon kill it. But if I don't pass the role, then it will surely die, or make an ass out of me. Saying another word, I introspectively gazed down at my self-esteem checklist. Reassurance is the other fallacy. You should already know. Would a surgeon go into surgery not knowing? A bull even has a goal in chasing the red flag. Yet, I continue, agreeing with my inner me that I am financially secure, attractive, and successful, according to the standards of what society deems, yet it shouldn't mean squat to Eve though. Firm in belief, I the barbarian saw that she became the proverbial winch that I would grab by the hair if I needed to.

The waitress, a middle-aged woman, had skin that started to cry like a raindrop strolling down a windowpane. Her stroll was a Slow but dull grind, and her Lucid energy was crying for change. Her smile and make-up could never cover age and her pinned up hair, naturally covered a swan's neck. She too, was the high school sweetheart. She was every local boys dream.

Chloe was holding up a valiant fight to resist. She made a cigarette castle that was strategically piled in the ashtray. They needed her to knock their edge down. They gave her edge. I contributed to the emotion. Something else was going on in her. To appease my guilt-and to nail to her intellect that I was the next best thing to Hawaiian bread-I ordered a blue concoction. The drink was strangely smooth and simply chilled. It poured from the spigot from afar, and I watched it crash atop the rocks. I ordered another, a Sapphire and tonic, which lies against a flawless backdrop of sky blue. It's a light and all too social drink. It was trendy, as I now describe it clearly, I find myself further describing Chloe during that time. I ordered her a house Cosmopolitan-whatever that was. After three sips, Chloe is shining the wonderful sunshine that reflects all light and rare stones, and she expressed a sunshine that would separate a true smile, from an act of humility. A movie star might insure this one. Her smile was one that I am a sucker for. Her smile, reminded me of a recurring dream. In the dream, I run frantically in the dark, searching for light, which could be that light that shines within or of the sun; any light. Only then would I realize that when the light shined, it was blinding; a blinding inner vision. It is but a light, but I would leave it again. I couldn't let her know that. Not through body language or conversation. I restated my name again, "Hello, I'm Theron Niles Jr."

Seductively, she batted her eyes and moistened her red lips, which all was delicately choreographed, and letting me know that she had dropped the red flag and replaced it with a white one. I thought she was about to leave.

Her voice was like a choir. "I'm Chloe Riles."

For the next hour, three blues tunes, and a few fiery sonatas later, we divulged. She was headed to LaCoste. Her Doctorate studies in Post Renaissance Art History waited for her to claim it. She longed to be a curator at a museum, at a hostel, or in a kindergarten classroom. Wherever there was art, and I told her that I was headed to Chicago on business as usual. I am feeling the buzz. My flight had just been called. I mentally trail off to the announcements of plane arrivals and departures. Beer goggles are pushing me to the brink as well.

I consider taking that older waitress. Her ass is round and firm. She can still keep it going. I can faintly hear her in the horizon. Her long hair was being unfolded, and her body easing down, and then down, and then down to her down pillow. I stepped away from the table, and fingered her in as she stood between the counter and the entryway to the bathrooms. She knew what I was fingering her for, for she also knew that I was once that high school guy who had a crush on her. Not in the physical, but on other levels. Yet she knew. I grabbed her by the hand, and stared her deep into her eyes as my story seemingly ran through her mind. I then kissed her, and she simultaneously releases her hair as she reaches out and shakes it a bit. She throws her arms around me. She turns and lifts her skirt, and at the same time dropping the garden covers and opening the green house doors that covered it all. How miraculous the green house smelt. It was like a vanilla and cinnamon potpourri, cut fresh from the Garden of Eden. She had seen this scenario once before as well. Her actions seemed premeditated, the same as a gardener, feeling today was the best day of the season to seed and prune, and plant the new floral stems. Perfectly orchestrated, she opens the tight wound bag, and props it just enough so the geranium bulb would hang at ninety degrees above the watering hose, and sparingly positioning it, just in case she would have to reach for it at anytime and use it to stimulate moisture. She was a trained horticulturalist; the wrong move or wrong fertilizer could ruin the geranium. Her grandmother taught her the trade years ago. I snap back to reality. Awakening to a smiling and staring Chloe.

"I must go; my plane is starting to board".

My grammar became formal. I was sort of ashamed of listening to it, and scared to hear it again. Chloe and I exchanged numbers and addresses. Like two business partners, meeting on a flight, finding similar interests and comfort in knowing that someone else who had a similar idea, could connect and capitalize on something financially rewarding. She gave me a kiss on my cheek, and it was gentle, a tad wet, warm, and it screamed at me to sexually react. She was intentionally getting it to come out. Her spirit whispered deep inside of me to grab and go. I started walking away and she waved, and I was left with only a memory, and a deep down feeling, as I reminisce on the feeling; I was headed to college while bidding a happy adieu. Bittersweet, yes, but I knew that when I returned, my family and I would celebrate. I snap back into reality again, and I find myself searching for my boarding pass, and finding a red scarf with lipstick.

"We'll definitely see each other again. Love, Chloe."

Devastated, I plopped into seat 4A and drifted to the sound of a stewardess moving my pillow. She too knew of my intentions, and I could tell that she was part of the mile high club, but it was too short a flight, and too crowded to get lost.

For five months, we shared conversations from eleven at night to four o'clock in the morning, and I would find myself panting, laughing, cringing at some points, and feeling envious. I found myself longing for her. We made the local phone carrier a few thousand dollars richer, creating conversations consisting of the goings-on's in both the States and LaCoste.

"Share with me the town news."

"The natives woke early. Go to the hills for occasional dancing. Live music concerts. They eat long lunches with strong wines and cheeses, coupled with fresh breads. Lone walks to the beach."

I never knew who "they" were. I assumed she was speaking of the locals.

My job and everything it offers me.

"Finance is a bore. Your quality of life is better." She would concur. We would both get a great laugh at her arrogance.

Despite these conversations, she would be open with me. Explaining how she wanted me.

"Make love to me. I adore watching a man's head between my legs, moving in circles." She moaned over the Atlantic, and I would listen loud and clear.

"I am cupping your head. Perform the duty as I'll then use you to pacify me, and twist you at all intervals and angles."

Conversations would get heavy. I had fallen for lust. Not an actual human being. I realized that I was starting a relationship with a woman off of image and prospect alone. Phone sex was a bitch. I loved everything about her.

Chloe's time in Europe was finally complete. Upon her move back to the States, with little discussion at all, we moved in together into a Brownstone in Brooklyn. It was four stops from the offices in Manhattan. The mortgage was fairly inexpensive. Chloe's artistic touch and my money, renovated the place. It was outfitted with contemporary amenities, filled with nicks and knacks, Armenian plates and rugs, with his and her furniture. I always wanted an expansive study, long enough to glare light upon an expansive book collection. I wanted tall shelves that would warrant using a ladder. I finally had my wish. Chloe, with a touch of luck and a few connections, assumed a position as a curator at Sotheby's, while teaching European Art History. Three years out of the Wilson Business School, I was part of the billion-dollar acquisition dream team that acquired the forth-largest luxury hotel chain in the world. Together, we would go on to acquire fifteen of the twenty largest hotel chains in the World, on behalf of billionaire suitors, who took other peoples money for the thrill of victory, and the chivalry of having another man by the throat, and refusing to let go, until that man slowly slides his heart across the table. Shy of my seventh year, I became a partner at Hockney and Associates Acquisitions, the biggest publicly traded brokerage firms on the continental United States. The music of my new life was definitely playing. I could hear the horns and pianos, coupled with synthesizers and string chords. It was the first time that I understood Bitches Brew. It even sounded like a long beat box or a continuous hand rhythm atop a newspaper dispenser. I believed that it was all of the music of my life. This music was a serenade of love and hope that my spirit had yet to explore, and it was topped off with passion and sensuality. The music was a build up, for a tragic burnout. I learned that I was a fool, blinded by the deft metal of my own fallacious music.

My family warned me. "You run into situations head first." You're a total and reckless abandonment.

My three closest friends warned me. "You plan on marrying an artsy type?" They thought that I was crazy. Love and lust doesn't recognize the voice of reason.

Consumed with pop culture and a pop reality, we wed, having a grand wedding. I flew over my immediate family and friends for this huge production. Clothing for the party, gifts for everyone, wine for the adults and wine for the children. Chloe's immediate family and friends also flew in. All cast upon the backdrop of the red setting sun in Belize. Belize was perfect, as it was relatively close and exotic, and a glance to the West, and you would constantly be bombarded with the site of picturesque hills and mountains. God spent a mere second creating it. How awesome is he? While looking over the rolling oceans, the music halted. Lightning Hopkins guided me down the dimly lit stairwell. The World chilled. I calmed my temporary insanity.

"By the beach", everyone exalted to me in unison.

Music bellowed in my mind. A music that reminded me of a time-I was poor in spirit-a lost soul. No money. I roamed the Earth. Not literally, but figuratively and metaphysically. I was that dust that I would wipe off on my grandmother's floor model television. It was a tubeless floor model television, which was supposedly appreciated for the big picture, yet used by the world as a drink holder or a bookshelf. I found myself as clear as I can remember that gutted out fish tank. Abused and ran ragged.

Approaching the beach, laughter from afar forced the blues of the moment to blast the harshest bravado-past insecurities. Being committed to someone reared its ugly head. I eclipsed the sand dune. I understood why, as I watched them sitting, side by side, and sharing wine and both in a drunken paradigm.

My friend, who was adamant enough to tell me, "don't get married" in the first place, was sharing a moment with my wife that I thought I should be sharing. I walked up, noticing this dumb ass friend since graduate school. I helped him to land a position at the office.

He tapped Chloe frantically on the hand, and with glazed eyes, she looked at me in a frozen state. She was stuck in that previous moment in time, as her face expressed the great disarray. I saw the large amounts of surprise. I thought everything about their time. I thought that the production -our wedding- atop of the hill was a grand one and I needed a release as well. Actions do speak louder than words.

"What's going on? It's time for our dance."

While giggling, she said, "We were talking about you and how much we both love you." Jason's face cracks with a laugh.

"Plus sweetheart, he scored some great buds!" It was supposed to be that innocent. I was supposed to be amused.

Jason smugly said, "Cool out brother, it's your wedding night. Take a hit."

Inner fires of hate burned. Scorching revelations and hexes ran through me. I glared at both of them, a wicked gander. The look was a perplexing and unsympathetic stare. I never witnessed my reflection so hateful. One that a harlot would not dare contradict. It was a pimp's rage. Nothing was positive about either looks. It was the first of many times in my life that I felt and applauded my anger. And rather than taking a hit, I took a hint. I later felt like I might have been over reacting, for maybe I had drunk too much wine. Maybe I was intoxicated-too much happiness. It was probably a mixture of every foul emotion that I understood, coupled with my own pride. Too much love. Though I was drunk, the candid portrait did not seem right. She reached for my hand. She failed while catching air and my bad intentions. He tried to reason. Confirming my over reaction. Yet I strolled away while kicking at the sand and scratching at my inner most revelations, while feeling sober, albeit sober. Eclipsing the hill and returning to the reception, I felt as though God had given me the ultimate blessing. My Family, who barely ventured past the mid Atlantic United States, and who were great grandchildren of sharecroppers were in Belize, witnessing the grace of God in another land. They didn't know it existed. No fighting and plenty of hand dancing. Chloe's family, though Mid-western, were good people. I enjoyed the moment. God was blessing me. By evenings end, Chloe, Jason and I were laughing together.

Back in New York, everything was peaceful. The music that forced Chloe and I together, returned with bebop trumpeters. Blue Note or Columbia even. Never take us apart it said. As our schedules started to get hectic, we spent less time together. The underlying smell of a bad situation was lurking. A serpent was creeping into Eden. Only a curious being would approach and offer a snake comfort. Only someone who knew nothing of a snake's cold slither, and comforting hiss could indulge in its mystique. He was the biggest swindler of them all. The fool finding out that he was a fool. I found my footing securely planted in the "fool's paradise."

Chloe began to stroll back to her lover from Lacoste, Alfaz Merc. I knew this. Each night, Chloe would un-shamelessly slide out of bed. Emulate her adulterer and slither down the back stairs and to the windowsill in the den where she remained captivated by his hiss; he was a friend. I believed her.

"The friend would disappear", I thought.

"Then again, it's healthy for her to have male friends."

High rains came and a lot of silent lightning. No thunder, but a smooth and gentle breeze. It was a tepid extreme. Each time, her subtle movement was a prelude to the repetitious exodus and I would follow suit, becoming their being. I was no longer a bull, but a bottom feeder, prying for a floor monger. Emulating the scenario, I would slide myself down to a tiptoe as I listened, learned, and planned my counterattack. They reminisced on the glare of the moonlight along the Seine, and Seasoned Merlot with seafood, breads, cheeses, and duck pate. She elaborated on the long nights of nakedness. They spoke of the occasions when they were arm in arm, gazing, while catching falling stars that dropped delicately between clasped hands. She glowed. The hiss took her to the ancient Ruins that were tall, old, and broken. I heard whispers of the archaic architecture in Prague, and how the buildings forcefully jutted atop the low clouds, yet romantically captivated them for and eternity, so it seemed. I sat there and died, as she coldly told him that she regretted marrying me, and even living in America once again.

"I was attracted to Theron's status more so than his personality. Combined, he does make an ideal husband, if you really want that type of husband."

"My heart is there Alfaz. It is amongst the long grass, cupping your heartbeat, kissing along the sun, and a breeze through and within the post office near your house. I am there."

Devastation turns to panic. I conceit to the glow that she radiated in front of me, while she talked to him, with an honest and caring aura. That same aura she shared with Jason. Retrospective clips, mental movies, all became piecemeal on advice that people had once tried to give me. Advice that was now prophetic. I had nowhere to run and hide. My decisions would now be my burden to bear. I fully blamed myself for my plight. I too was committed for the wrong reasons.

My inner-conscience said it best, "I should listen more."

The most important moment of this whole experience, the entire lesson of what was needed for me to learn, flashed before me. I murmured to myself, *the fool.* Despite your money, your status, your kindness, and your Love for others, you still are susceptible to playing *the fool*, or the jester. These thoughts force me to think of myself as an underling or the Narcissist. In theory, I am the epitome of the Bull.

I started to withdraw from my life around Chloe. For months after the ordeal, I would whisper to myself *My Wife*. Before and after prayer, during happy thoughts that would surface for whatever reason, I would weakly say her name. Lust and her second cousin love had me blind folded, and like the Sagittarius, I was Smitten for pure beauty. This woman would slide out of bed, and slink down the staircase and would continue this pattern every Tuesday and Thursday for a few months. Each time, her exodus was too gentle for a sleeping person, and too delicate for someone going to get water. I would feel her move out of bed. I would roll the other way. Between my work and her whatever, we fell. The branches of iniquity plucked me off and showed me my own fears in Technicolor surrealism. From the cloud nine high, I began a descent in which I took a long glance of my surroundings of cherubs, cherry trees, green grass and my once prevalent wings. I found myself plucked like I was the cherry, left to drop, all the while seeing myself descending, falling, and finally I hit the ground-broken. There was no way to back up, and I was nowhere near that level. The marriage was over. I dared not ask whom she snuck downstairs for. I knew. She most assuredly knew that I knew. If only I knew better, but better would not help me. My love for her left on that cold night, which was the same night the serpent whispered into her ear, and forced the truth out of me. The blindfolds, the left eye, Love, and the right eye of Lust, were both unsuspecting and confusing and both allusive at the same time. I looked at her as lust would look at any undeserving woman. Not worth my time. No hassle. No love. Dry desolate garbage was always available at work, and the money, the forgiving hooker she is, once again became my sexual intimate companion and passion. She's my comfort and my refuge. It's funny how the one thing that you do for money turns and becomes the variable that placates your own need to live.

For extracurricular prowess and to show my face, for months I would stay behind at the office and schmooze. The "League fraternity" that had formed at the firm was a peculiar bunch. I nestled in the corner with some of the other professional staffers, and would share a laugh and a smile. Even a good time was hard fought. Even after the aged whiskey. If anything, the atmosphere, with a cigar, bred envy and mild hatred for everyone not me. Men with real historical money-actually having conversations consisting of Wall Street, vacation places that the layman could never feel comfortable venturing to-sitting around with the same people for hundreds of years having the same conversations. It seemed that the common goal amongst these men were to make sure that they in fact would have those conversations five hundred years from that evening.

Squash tournaments and crew regattas were nothing but "a moment to sip a good cup of java, and watch a real team sport."

Women were average. Dating situations arranged through supper clubs. The majority of their schools had those. Nothing changed for these men. Life mapped out for them from the moment of conception. I took home a portion of the money that they would make bringing in clients. I envied them. I don't have a handful of black men with whom I could sit around and enjoy life for what we know, sharing the perspective that we were bred from. Instead, I have to fight assimilation. My everlasting fight becomes a rage against the machine, and I remain seen, powerful, yet detached. I am neither black nor white. I just know that I am.

I remember though. I wasn't alone in leaving behind my sometimes hard to swallow past. That experience did not come in networking in the office, but came with falling in love with the most perfect woman who was deaf to deception. She was unshakeable, and always willing to fight for love. She was thoughtful and trustworthy. Lindsay had short and toned legs. She was from Philadelphia. Ran track at Temple University during her undergraduate studies. Lindsay and I met at the Wilson school as second semester students. Lindsay shoulders were always tight, yet always inviting. She was always elegant, even devoid of competition. After a jog I would gladly massage her; she was soft and her skin supple. It was nice and round for an athletic female. Had she sat it down for even a second, it would have been the perfect bottom. Lindsay and I would find a way to Central Park; rather it was a sunny day, or some rainy days. We would frolic under the hazy sky, while staying intimately embraced in the falling rain. The moment was calm, the sentiment was fitting, and love was what we were wrapped in, yet never spoke it. We just felt it. We would take pictures and enjoy the day, discussing life as descendants of underprivileged, middle rung black people, whose parents barely made enough moves to turn things around. She would expand upon her experiences as an athlete at the collegiate level. I would share with her the sights and people I had encountered while studying abroad in both the United Kingdom and Japan.

She was quick witted, and full of Politics. Our reality was historical. It was different than any other experience. Never be a square. Never walk with your nose raised high. Success is momentary, and dependent upon your right place and your right time, and in order to succeed, one must avoid those wrong decisions. Never turn your back on the people who helped you get to where you will be as a professional, but mainly as a human being. We were inseparable and second natured and we never thought to leave one another. We couldn't possibly think about marriage. Too many career ambitions and too many social morals seemed to set us adrift in different directions as corporate acquisitions pays extremely well. Classical music would have to be the means for mental survival. Lindsay was working towards child advocacy and eventually opening her own free clinic on financial management. She expected short and reasonably difficult days. She needed to learn how to truly appreciate Al Green and Otis Redding. Due to our hectic CPA exam schedules and moving arrangements, we didn't speak much the last four months of school. Instead, life became a slow guitar strum from Jobim, as the reality that we knew became the melody of our last moments.

"Destiny involves you being prepared for whatever."

"Simply put", I thought and reflected for a moment.

Thoughts of never leaving this woman surfaced through my conscience. I kissed her on her shoulders. The feelings were mutual. We were ruining a lasting and dependent relationship-one caring for the Love of community, the other for the Love of prestige and money. Because we were parting ways, I had already broken the creed -by taking the first acquisitions job that kicked me a little rhythm, and showed enough money, and interest. My music of life officially changed. Classical it was. My reality inherently changed as well.

After the schmoozing sessions at the office, I would return home to the smell of Asiago, French Opera, and nearly melted candles.

A letter that usually read, "Honey art opening tonight in the village, dinner's on the table, Chloe."

It has been five years to date. I brazenly walked onto the beaches of Chloe Riles, allegedly loving her in the name of Holy matrimony, which technically, was my dumb ass confusing love with lust. I strolled from the office through Manhattan, admiring the towering buildings, swank places to eat and doorways to sleep. Everything was a mere blur. The World seemed to pace at a higher rate than thought. Nothing was manageable. Not even a coffee shop. The fiscal quarter was nearly over, and my time at the office dwindled, which was good for me, yet bad for the firm, and my days were short and unthankful. I can almost say that it was unrewarding. As I returned home nightly, I walked up to a bottle of wine, some smelly cheese, pasta and an appropriately placed note. On one of those evenings, I found my salvation through an old crate of records; some Motown, Blue Note, Casablanca, and Sony. In my dark, musty, dry, lonely, smelly, hole of an attic, classics were everywhere. All of the "War" classics, especially *Deliver the Word*. "Earth, Wind and Fire's" *Gratitude* album was there. Isaac Hayes' *Hot Buttered Soul* was lying there, and there was salvation and hence instant rejuvenation. My soul was longing, yet gleaming, and raining positive energy. It also placed my soul in its rightful place. It was Friday when I received e-mail from *lady luck*. My life would never be the same. It was Lindsay.

I tried not to get too excited, for I hadn't spoken to Lindsay for sometime and this contact could mean anything. I hoped that it shied far from death and was devoid of heartbreak. I also thought happily of her possibly not succumbing to the paradigm that she anxiously chose. For the first time in a really long time, it felt as though the sun had shined just enough to get me to smile and enjoy this feeling of excitement. Lindsay e-mailed a time for us to make contact using instant messaging. She had a daughter, Gene', and had married a screenwriter. He spent his days cleaning the house, cooking food, running errands, and hanging with a couple of big wigs in Hollywood. We wrote of old times and how we once walked hand in hand without a care in the world and swinging joyously into the wind. Not caring about the here in now, then and there. Caring only about the energy we exchanged through the bases of our palm. That energy would gently travel from each other's heart, and each pulse felt like one. Once again in my life, Love was real and the world revolved around Lindsay and me. My workload soon returned to its normal pace so Lindsay and I couldn't spend as much time online. We decided to e-mail each other every other day. For weeks, I began to hear a music that I had lost long ago. That music was similar to a constant thump and dragging of the drumstick across the snare, a march towards what, I never knew. It was something new that I had not experienced. Lady Luck would write and we relayed conversations as if we were that one silent beat. A solid heartbeat I heard, which equaled a thump for a send and two thumps for a return. Four thumps when the return was simultaneous. Time moved on like time usually will, and Lindsay and I failed to connect. I would e-mail her and instant message her frequently, but I would never receive a response. For weeks thereafter, rather than schmoozing, I would hit a café or a bar and catch whatever live music at any bar that I came across. That feeling of renewal and getting out, soon died down. Once again, I became the workaholic and reclusive, buried within the superficial matters of my life as an financial manager-worrying about other folks money- and a lonely soul.

During my recluse of sorts, I did manage to salvage a few hours to get out and create some type of *jazz* of my own. If only the World could hear. Usually on Friday's I would hit the movies mid-day. Catch a new release. I even ventured out enough to delve into Feng Shui placement lessons. On Friday, I decided that I would search for some toys to enjoy while in my recluse. I was in the mood for learning new recipes. I went to Little Italy and visited a couple of other ethnic boroughs and took some black and white photos. Personal photos of others are the free cinema reels of the social human. Photography is by far one of the best stress relievers and creative projects that one could choose to do. Being that I hadn't taken any decent photos in two years, this session was a real treat. My thoughts ventured to develop them while smelling fresh cilantro; lamb chops, simmering atop cous cous. This dinner was a decent reward for a Gordon Parks enthusiast.

I walked up the stairs, past the hymen, deep within the oak doors. I grabbed the mail. How disappointing it had been to not hear from Lindsay again. And though we were on *the ousts,* I would have loved to share my work of the day with Chloe. We hadn't slept in the same bed for weeks. Lindsay, in mere e-mail messages, had resurrected my soul. I was a Phoenix, living quickly, aging gracefully, burning myself, and dying a day, resurrected by love tomorrow. Where's the love but in Lindsay? She rushed the needed blood of righteousness to my conscience. I missed her.

In the mail, I found the usual subscriptions and bills. GQ, Financial Weekly, Mademoiselle, Antiques, The Robb Report, Men's Health, Vibe, the phone bill and a couple of credit card bills, and a lively decorated envelope. My self-loathing turned into momentary euphoria. The envelope showed red lips devouring a red sucker, with a gorgeous hand to follow. It was driven insanity.

The title on the attractive envelope spelled my name perfectly in calligraphy. My subscription to Playboy had finally paid off. Maybe it's a party invite the Playboy mansion. Hardly! I situated the groceries. I bolted to the bathroom. Plopping myself onto the toilet seat. I opened the envelope. Paris lurched out and grabbed my attention. Paris was this perfume that an old friend of mine loved. Vintage, inexpensive, and created an adventure to find it. Lindsay it was. She had stopped writing. She was going through her own personal nightmare.

"Arrived home a day early from an Education Rally in San Diego and was met with a candle lit table, two half eaten venison chops, pureed potatoes and a few Snifters of Cognac (Louis XVI). I walked upstairs to the master bedroom. It was full of lit candles." Upon entering the bedroom she was horrified. She found her nude husband, snugly sleeping in their bed with a man.

She went on to say that she left the house disgusted and filed for a divorce the very next day. She loved this man and gave him so much and wondered why he did this to himself and his family. She said the reality of her situation was unbelievable. I loved Lindsay. In the face of adversity, she managed to hold on to reality, by searching and finding a silver lining.

Two lines later, "I thought something was up."

"I never dated light skinned men, because they are too high maintenance and are never quite right."

She was planning on moving back to Philadelphia with her mother for a short time. Gene' would stay with her mother while she vacationed in December.

She finished her letter, "Thank you for never leaving."

My heart dropped below my beltline. I knew that I had physically left her and had been away from her for a few years. Her understanding was well beyond comprehensive parameters. Maybe I am still the type of man I was years ago. She expected me to be this man I am.

"I will find you when the chords of life will allow us to converge on the Miles Davis levels of Love and experience. I had to throw that in there

Theron. I know you enjoy this cryptic and poetic stuff."

I folded the letter up, blinking back into reality, and shook my head, wiped my eyes and said a prayer for Lindsay's situation.

The envelope from Lindsay showed a sucker. This sucker would be synonymous with the life I had been living.

I opened the credit card bills. Nearly $13,000 had been amassed in the last month. Description of the charges; "two roundtrip tickets (Northwest Airlines) from JFK to Charles de Gaulle-Paris, Versace Boutique (Milan), Cruise passes."

The never-ending list went on. Right then and there, my heart fell to such despair as I realized that the 2:00 a.m. phone calls had blossomed into a dependent relationship.

I ran downstairs, feeling no need to slide. It's funny how real fury can change a man. I went from a slithering serpent to that enormous creature with four hooves, while frantically lunging for Johnny Walker Blue Label. My thoughts would be to get high and get high quickly. I sat a chair by the door, Scotch in hand, waiting and breathing heavily from each nostril. I imagined the depth of my eyes, and how they must have looked as blank as two coals and devoid of life, yet full of loss and despair. I was waiting for the red flag to swing once again. Come in, I said to myself. I dare you. Each of my heartbeats from the left and right ventricles crashed against my breastbone quicker and quicker, as my soul was actually excited by the possibility of confrontation. The anticipation of whatever may be. I had no idea what time she came. Friday's I avoided home. Until after nine o'clock. Maybe I would rent a room. Johnny Walker played his part. Blood rushed to my head, as adrenaline was pumping through my palate faster than my heart murmurs. I mentally conceit to the bedroom. It was at that very moment that I heard a conversation in French. I retract to the door, a little alarmed, yet holding myself together; my mind started sprinting towards the closet. I conceited long ago that in protecting myself in the Jungle, I would wield her, summoning her protection. Forty-five Smith and Wesson snug nose, its license and hollows was snugly waiting. God had a hand on me. Adrenaline slowed, palate still wet. A voice of reason was shouted from left field. Calmly, I sat back down, grasping the analytical and metaphysical responses for my actions and the truth behind Chloe moving on with her life. My work forced me to spend less time with Chloe. We were two people who were infatuated with the idea of marriage, and not the actual commitment associated with marriage. It was over. I made the decision and suffered its consequences. I felt better after my revelation.

She walks through the door, radiant and aglow. This garden eel, a pale man, accompanies her with his stringy hair mushrooming over his shoulders, while his tapered tight jeans covered the scales. His loafers turned up in the front, as if feet weren't inside the shoe at all. Maybe it was a pair of my old ones. I too played the role of the serpent many times in my life, and up until that moment. With all of strength that I could muster, that strength which is of me and created within, I yelled. Chloe panicked. Her glow turned to gloom, as her façade was ghostly, and from human being she transposed to her suitor-a snake. She erupted into tangents about my working habits. Jealous towards other women who husband's had taken them out on the town. Her points were valid, albeit moot. I alluded to the fact that she would rather look cool walking through the City rather than building a lasting marriage.

She audaciously boasted, "Alfaz is poor, but was what she needed in a man. "Alfaz and I lay in the grass, while catching the breeze. We hold hands as we stroll through the park watching kid's play from afar, while admiring the street merchants and musicians. Alfaz's daughter actually appreciates my company. She calls me mommy."

In utter disgust, I let all of my frustrations go. "What are you talking about? What does all this have to do with you and me?

I then said, "Don't answer. Pay this credit card bill. Gather your things. Meet me at my office tomorrow to sign a divorce motion." She would now have a reason to tell her friends how much of an ass I was.

"Make sure that *'Moulin rouge'* over there comes to my office as well with a new pair of loafers and maybe a cooler haircut." I staggered down the stairs and into the dark as blind, as the World continues to swirl me around, and similar to an ice cube in a glass. Everything around me is out of control. The matador, a brute warrior has stuck me across the shank and deep into my heart. He pushed me clean into the street leaving his red cloak wrapped around my horns. Jewish neighbors rescued me. Never would I have thought it. They petition to keep me out of here, and they were gentle, understanding, and sympathetic. The Markowitz's were giving. I lunged for the taxi door. I spoke enough for the driver. They repeated the sentiment for me. They both extended their hands to me, forcing their ivory tree limbs through the half-closed window. Music I had never heard. Their eyes told me a lifelong tale in two seconds. In silence, and through their eyes, they communicated that they regretted not knowing me. We all shared a moment of hope. I managed to secure a double for the night at the Marriott. It was cold and I was alone with no money, no pictures, and no food. I can recall lying in that hotel room with my indifferent self and me. The next day with headache and all, I asked Steven Cole Krowowitz - a bi-racial dude in the legal department- to help me out. He was long faced, light skinned, with small glasses. He wore conservative clothes, dark pants, a white shirt and a dark tie. A dispenser with tissue seemingly floated beside him wherever he went. He was humming a tune pumping from somewhere beyond the walls. Until that day, Stevie was the squarest Negro that I knew. Reserved, understanding, yet forthright and deeply troubled, he glided towards the door and closed the door. He looked into my eyes, grimacing at the reflection within. "Brother", he said as he wiped his nose and adjusted his glasses atop the crown of his nose, "my father told me that a woman could make you or break you. It's up to you to choose which reason you love her for. To make you better, or to break you down and leave you." He smiles and wipes his nose once again, "Theron, all is well that ends well." He strolled away humming a tune, sniffling down the hall. From that day, no longer was Stevie a sellout Uncle Tom, nor square dude to me. Stevie was and had been my brother.

Chloe and her peasant lover left the office and he was wearing a new pair of loafers. She was wearing a mole-haired ensemble with a red hat. The most distinguishable accessory was her smile. It was radiant and beautiful. The same feeling I had staring at my mother as they laid her to rest. She was finally happy and reunited with those that loved her for her.

Sitting at the hotel amongst the emotional rubbish and aftermath of my tryst with Lust, I thought about how I would survive without what I considered success; money, prestige, material. Success is as bad as fear. One hinges on the other. Without either, you cannot attain nor keep. Interpersonal skills, eroded over the years leave you with a new starting point. I am still young. I also thought about Stevie. This guy and I were connected beyond the parameters of the profession. We were both black and in a World of the minority, and seemingly hated by all, and alienated by society on a whole. We shopped at Saks. Dressed and spoke in a certain way. The title of Black men of prominence placed us out of the ghetto. The suburbs of Black America, the gray areas in which whites still think that we're benefactors of affirmative action. Blacks think that we're *Uncle Toms*. We began to believe anything. My understanding is perfectly clear; I was at the glass ceiling of social and racial equality. I was fed up with playing a part. There was such a thing. No need to renew my lease.

For eight years I had been wasting my life working for wealth, and living for mediocrity. I went to work, cleaned my desk, settled my stock options and resigned from my post. Why battle, when wealth is not enough of a motive? I would take my closest friends advice. Forget about the *money* field, I named. Forget about unchangeable circumstances. Selah.

It's June 14, 2000. Four years to date, my marriage. Nine years since embarking upon my journey in the *money field*. Standing in the empty brownstone I realized that everything had come full circle. Once again, I was alone. While waiting for Chloe to sign some closing documents and to collect a few of our collective remnants, I bounced a ball back and forth against the hollow walls. As I glanced around the room, I silently cried over losing the bookcase, the ladder, and my own study.

I planned to stay with my mother for a while down in Maryland. Enjoy my family's company. Take an extended vacation. Three hours late, Chloe *"the peasant lover"* arrived with one of her art friends-Simena. I intentionally flirted with her and passed my information, while listening to pleas of no malice from Chloe. I never was mad at her. I am mad at the dude that I stare at everyday. Never expressing that to her, but letting her take her self through the inferno.   I extended my hand and shook hers.

Christmas was a day gone. Heading to Costa Rica and then to Jamaica. Maybe return ready to stake out real estate, close to the water, hopefully three steps from a beach in a chair, facing the coast. The Setting sun would be my television. Costa Rica has a lot of Rain Forests and cool breezes, coupled with vibrant people. It was New Year's Eve as my time in Costa Rica went effortless and quickly. I had Ochos Rios on my mind.

Jamaica. I stay at this quaint little time-share, which is far from the hedonists, close to the natives, and reclusive enough to be left to rest. Off of the airplane, and walking to the property car, I was swerving with the swaying trees, as the sun was stroking my ego. The water was like Eve's water hole. I requested Rum Punch.

"No punch man. I have Just Rum!"

So this driver-a tall dude, as dark as night with hair that ran down his back like serpents; I think he was a Rasta- had a love for Depeche Mode- and I siphoned rum from the bottle, until we got to the property. Buddy Wailers was now playing at this point. Under the clear sky, was the ocean breeze and I was now returned to the perch I once knew, cloud twelve this time, admiring all beings from afar. I was a mile from the resort, gazing in astonishment of the people genuinely enjoying themselves. Maybe it was the rum. For whatever reason, I requested information on renting yachts. I purchased a sarong for whatever might happen on the beach. Flying down from my self-induced high, I feel like every motion is effortless. Patience is no longer a virtue but my call to arms.

"Damn, no personal cosmetics!"

"First things first", I spoke out and into action.

Getting dressed and walking to the front desk was murderous and insane even. Not a motion of my own as I felt like I floated and was attached to strings. The puppet master was phenomenal, and cool, calm and allowing me to live without care. Elder emotions resurfaced, and these emotions were deep ones that went far down to the dark part of these blue waters, and well beyond the coral and atop the water grass. Beyond the fables and tales of what was, I caught a glimpse of her;

white, slightly high shoes and her foot and connected heel of this woman must have been pumiced down to tantalizing sucking bliss. Her calf muscle was firm. She was as ripe as Adam had witnessed those on Eve's body. The backs of her legs, tanned equally as the rest of her body. Through her knotted white skirt, you could see that her ass was as ripe as the Carolina peaches from yesteryear. That pie was raised under the quiet care of a baker and was readily waiting to be bitten into. This cloud of tanned flesh was left marinating in the finest supple oils and inched through the elastic of the white bathing suit. Making a halfhearted effort of holding it all in. Bikini topped. Shoulders tense. Instincts told me that she yearned for the right firm grip to rub them the right way. Her hair was manicured like Dorothy Dandridge's in Carmen, and those winding angles of her wonderful neck was a blissful sight. Slumber from years of desolate garbage was finally behind me. She turned. I smiled. She glided down the stairs. I begged all of Heaven and all of Earth for her to look up and smile. Lindsay raised her head ever so slightly. Not wanting too much attention, she recognizes me with her eyes wide.

"Theron?"

The love of the World once again, played in our honor.

"Yes, Lindsay!" I exalted.

With a quivering tongue and a weeping soul, she ran towards me. Her shaking hands and knees were mine. I caressed her soft, sweat, body. I smelled her hair, staring at her to make sure it was not an oasis, or sun stroke. It was Lindsay, and I would long no more.

Caressed until the Hedonists found our oasis riveting, the sun was right above hour heads. An eternity passed as we slowly kissed without lips, and without sound. We felt just a heartbeat and the same music.

Frankie Vali's *I Can't Take My Eyes of You* meant something.

Stevie Wonder's *Another Star*, bellowed throughout the climatic corridors of my spirit. Smokey Robinson's Quiet *Storm* blew over us.

"I Love you", gently fell off of the both of our lips.

I created the word *Epiphany*.   I rediscovered music.

Reality Check:
The Ultimate Dose of Reality

I was listening to Frankie Beverly and Mazes *Golden Time of Day*, just because that golden time of day was upon me. I could actually feel the positive energy penetrating into the caverns of my eyes. Staring out at the sunset, realizing that it was still able to blind me. Not able to hide its vulnerabilities or its blemishes. I conceit to the fact; not many people know themselves. I am speaking of those who will never make an attempt to explore one self and meticulously arrange my emotions and thoughts. Feeling like *that something* was missing. I call that missing item or the hole in the wall, as I would prefer phrasing it, *the search after the search.*

From time to time, I find myself sitting atop scattered sands of delicate intricacies that are so colorful, so rare, that I can only see them. Neither explanations nor description could attempt to draw a general etch for a commoner's understanding, yet never quite explaining to the eyes and hearts present, its glory. But there, the euphoric phantasm of the most beautiful thing you could not fathom, even if your last breath depended upon it, lay my childhood, adolescence and hopeful manhood-for these days, manhood is a rarity as boyish tendencies are kept in arms reach. Hoping that my fight is as valiant as my mother's, as introspective as my father's, which is enough to deem me a man worthy of more than a rat race. For whom, I sometimes wonder. The question is all too relative. I hope for selfish reasons. I collect. Poke. Explore. Running into the *search after the search*, I find myself. Still not knowing what other realms there remains to discover. For the very first time in my life, I stand at the crossroads. The meaning of crossroads; literally sitting yourself in the middle of your own mental fairway, patiently waiting and watching for a physical sign from God or maybe a psychological sign from God through your conscience. It points you in the *right* direction. *Right,* meaning what is the best way for you to travel. God made every man in his image and gave every man a distinct mind. God also gives everyone his or her own standard, and in turn, their own right direction.

This soul search is a deciding path of sorts, ultimately leading to a destination that I am ignorant of. I have never seen nor searched there. Mazes' *Happy Feelings* usually brings me to and rather picking one path to follow, I sit down amongst all of these emotions, feelings and thoughts, and the Faith directs me. I listen to the breezes of the Word of God. Whether in the wind or in a dream, I rest assured that it does come.

Nothing that I encounter in life will be as bad, for a lot of people experience worse. I have a roof over my head, food on the table, and a peace of mind that evolves on a daily basis. People in this World, have little to no freedoms, no feelings, and no insights on their own life. They don't even have a clue to what they need to get through this day-to-day struggle. I enjoy daily, the ultimate epitome of *personal luxury*. Personal luxury-not as commanding as the word *luxury*-but it is however, my own and to my liking, and hence my *personal luxury*. Sure, I am viewed by most in a strange light, and hence I remain shunned. The same ears would listen to me if I were filthy rich. But because I enjoy the subtle lifestyle that I have attained, that becomes a social improbability. I have a functioning family-whatever that is-dancing a jig to see me happy. They allow my weird ass to be a part of their reality. Someone has no family and no one to sacrifice for their betterment. If you have been in an instance in life where you have extracted yourself from family, then you will understand. And if you haven't extracted yourself from family, the time will come when it is necessary to do so. Not because you don't feel deeply for them. You do need them. Human growth will force you to expand mentally. Independence within self - both physical and mental independence-is the key and ultimately the redeemer.

The *search after the search* is as beautiful as the search for you. Choose to make it that far. Realize that the *search after the search* isn't a search at all. It is life in its present tense. Hence, let this be a guiding light for some and a refresher for others. I offer you the first of many Reality Checks.

Story 3:

For the Love of Bojangles

(A Ghost of Mr. William)

"It's wild!"

"What's wild?"

"The situation is wild because of the fact that the both of us have been married, divorced, and are still here."

"Girl, I don't think it's wild. Better yet, I would hope that you would have used functional as an adjective for our situations." Appropriate, justifiable would be the two other "ideal" words that I would use to further describe our present state of being."

"And what, are we supposed to be dead, or disenfranchised or something?

"Well no. At this point in life, you couldn't have told me twenty years ago that we would both be married and divorced for one. College and graduate school graduates for two. Kid-less, man-less, and so entangled in the *corporate world* that we fail to even recognize that we are literally kissing the base of that clairvoyant ceiling."

"Maybe you don't care."

"You know what? I dare not open that can of worms right now."

"Hmmm, you probably shouldn't."

"But seriously, we have topped out. I mean, maybe not as much in that we still get "carded" when we go to clubs, and the fact that older men still want to be our sugar daddies. But we've topped out in our profession and we are used goods in any social setting worth breaking into, because of our divorce baggage."

"Well maybe by your standards, because Glo, you have always been very hard on yourself. This kitty got a good two hundred thousand more miles before it is due for inspection. And what is wrong with sugar daddies. Your ass did not complain when old man (Dr.) Hopkins and (Professor) *Viagra* Simpkins took us to the Greek Isles last fall."

"Why did you have to go there? I thought that man was going to overdose on Viagra."

"Hmmm, girl you are not right!"

"What are you doing tonight anyway?"

"Going home and cleaning up. Ever since I came back from Taiwan on that merger deal with, I haven't had a chance to clean up."

"I know that's right."

"Well girl, I'm going out and getting me a drink or something. Maybe pick me up a bar slut or something."

"Now you know you are not right!"

"But girl, that slut's money from billing that overtime all week just might!"

"Girl, call me, alright?"

"Alright."

Hi, my name is Gloria. My friend Summer is crazy. We grew up together. We make a conscious effort to get together and talk for a few hours everyday. We meet at this park where this homeless guy Buddy, provides us with the commentary on the latest news on the street.

Sometimes he confronts the passions of the buses and how majestic the smog looks when the diesel fuels smoke blow past his bench. Other times, Buddy presses the envelope and sits down. Taking Summer and I on a descriptive impression of the world. You would be surprised to find out that Buddy has a lot mores street sense that the majority of people with college degrees- those who consider themselves to be professionally educated. The pigeons, in Homeless Pigeon Park as we have dubbed it, fly directly above our heads. As the sun catches the creatures at an angle, you can understand why pigeons are majestic creatures. They can fly!

Through the low grasses, the squirrel's tails are happily bobbing as they chase their cousins amongst the city fray.

Sum and I usually discuss men, and all of the crap we women put up with in dealing with them. I love playing my role around Sum. I have always been the sane one. I never was too promiscuous, except in college maybe. And Sum, well lets just say that every man I have introduced her to, comfortably asks me, "How is can I get Sum?" I don't mean to put her business out there. She is after all my best friend. She has no inhibitions and uses the fact to enjoy all of the pleasures in life. Glamour, Sex, wealth, travel and games- not to be mistaken by board games-for she is the epitome and total embodiment of an independent woman of the millennium. Since Sum and Rob divorced, her sex life has increased. Not because she loves sex-though love is an understatement-but because she was sexually suppressed in her marriage. When the marriage was over, she made up for lost time. The negative equals a positive of sorts.

Speaking of marriage and men, it's this gentleman in my building by the name of Theron Niles, Jr., who I am quite smitten with. He's never quite doing one thing at a time. He is a tap dancer, spoken word poet, musician, father-his son is mulatto, a vintage music collector, photographer and a novelist. Published and all. The guy even had the audacity and talent to earn his MBA and was quite successful for several years. I found all of this information out one night when he first moved into the building.

I was preparing a few business proposals that were due the following day. The upstairs unit had been vacant for several months. The owners, Mr. and

Mrs. Sollensky moved on, literally. Both of them are eighty-two, and couldn't maintain the apartment without assistance. Their children moved them into a nursing home, which if I had anything to do with wouldn't have happened. I have a keen distaste for nursing homes. Nursing homes are like holding pens for the old aged to pass on. At that age, who needs another form of pacification? I say let me live my last days at peace both mentally and physically and with my significant other-if I had one-at my home. They were a nice couple that boasted about their fifty-seven and a half years of marriage. They were also very loud to be so old. I would hear old Fred Astaire and Rosemary Clooney tunes bellowing through the floor ever other night around 10:00 p.m. I would sometimes fall asleep with my laptop in my lap, to the slow mellow shuffles of aged affection and love. They were a happy couple, something that I sorely lack-happiness.

The Sollensky's were moved out and it was euphoric to not hear a sound every night above me, though it made my evenings that much lonelier. I was nearing the end of the proposal when I heard an enormous thud around 8:30 p.m. on the hardwood. First I ignored it, but then the thud got louder and quicker and so obnoxious that I put some slippers on and marched upstairs, only to meet an open door, with a horn blaring (unbeknownst then, it was Cole Porter's horn) and this man dancing.

"Theron Niles," he said. "Sorry about the noise. You must be Gloria?" He extended his hand, but he was too new for me to oblige, plus I was nervous because I was wondering how he knew my name.

"I tried to contact you to inform you that I would be tapping on Tuesday's around this time. The landlord gave me a list of all of the owners, and I made contact with all of them except you. I do apologize", he said.

"Will you forgive me?" he replied, with all of the intent of a small child, who was asking his mom for forgiveness.

Before I could say a word, he began to start tapping again while itemizing himself to me. He first tells me all of his vitals and all of his hobbies and interests. Mind you, he was doing this while tap dancing. He seemed interesting enough to listen to, plus I was a mere twenty minutes or so from finishing the proposal and the break was very much needed. Theron kept tapping, and while doing so he started to explain to me in action, what styles of tap dancing he was performing.

"Jimmy Doyle & Harland Dixon introduced this style of tap dancing," as he seemed to buck a bit. Like a wild horse would buck its hind legs toward the sky, but in a simple and tamed motion. He then said that a guy by the name if Bubbles or something to that effect, developed a more syncopated and slower style, which he began to show me, as the Compact Disc changer switched, and a familiar sound that my dad played to me before bed flourished. It was Duke Ellington's crew. They did a little something to his living room. The towering ceilings seemed as if the band might be jamming out directly above Theron and me.

I'm sitting on the floor at this point, and Theron continues to tell me about all of these other tap dancers, meanwhile he's tapping and demonstrating to me their actions.

Finally, a half an hour later, and a few splinters in my hand, he said, "but the man who I envy the most, and patent my tap after is Mr. Bojangles Williams."

At this point he grabs my hand and pulls me onto my feet and into his place. I am a bit taken aback but it seemed as if from this orientation and school lesson of sorts, I had become totally comfortable with this man. The door was wide open, and Ethal Hart was a nosey one across the hall. She wouldn't allow anything to happen to me.

"Mr. Bojangles was the man", he said, with his pearly teeth gleaming in my direction. It was around this time that I found my now bare feet atop his leather tap shoes, and he was staring at me directly in my eyes with a passionate blaze that I had never seen in a man before. A seriousness that reminded me of my father when I did something out of place, he whispered, "Mr. Bojangles' style of tap dancing is how I tap dance and how easy yet elegantly, I live my life. And just like that, it was if the wind had twirled me out of the apartment by the hand, and he calmly said to me, "Glo, if I may call you that, we'll have plenty of time to vibe out, and I do apologize for the noise." He then eases his door shut and the music completely stopped.

After that night, Theron and I connected on several levels. One in particular was that he always asked me female advice after something good or bad provoked his creativity. For advice, I would always reassure him that, "it isn't you, it's the woman. Trust me." As if I really knew how he treats a woman. I must admit that Theron's soul runs deep. Abysmal, should you consider that his presence demands that you be nothing less than gentle and kind around him. He only allows you into his world as much as you believe that you are in. I can easily compare his persona to my life as a divorcee and career woman. I couldn't do right in my marriage, simply because I didn't become the woman that my husband envisioned. As a career woman, I allow the business that consumes me to limit my growth within the field. I will never go beyond the throngs of the glass rooftop of my career arena, because I allow a group of men to pacify me with ambitious agendas and positive ideals. Those men then dangle the realization that they want another man in my position. And those men want this. Not because of my education or anything surrounding the parameters of the professional environment. They want another man in my position merely because I am of the opposite sex-womanhood in corporate America to men, equals incompetence for some reason. I can go no further in this world. Subconsciously, this is why I am so intrigued by Theron. Theron lives his life emotionally, how I live my life physically. I can go no further with the things I want to control, and women can go no further with Theron unless they are completely open, spiritually and mentally.

There are many different levels to Theron if you ask me. It seems to me from lengthy conversation and moments that there is something that he hides at the core of his energy. In Theron's case, the inferno would be his heart and soul. Somehow, you know there is true love within him, except to find that love, you have to descend many flights of emotional and spiritual stairs. Most of the stairs are emotional. Getting there, to the core, is what forces people, men and women, to walk away. Who has the patience to go through all of that bullshit to get to a person's heart and soul, with the possibility that the person doesn't want you there in the first place? Even though I say that I would never get married again, I would marry this man-or at least give him a piece! And the reason why I have come to such a realization is because I have been patient and resilient in getting to understand and know him. And through this process of acclamation, I openly eliminated all of the sexual magnetism that existed or could remotely exist between the two of us. That's where most women went wrong, I thought. They didn't know how to perfect his game. I know Theron. He didn't want a casual love or a casual friend. He wants another life from which he can extract and offer inspiration. I know that and strongly believe that I can be his inspiration. And should that happen, soon after there would come his time and life, which ultimately would equal true love. I firmly believe this.

"Let me get on in this building." Gloria gingerly creeps up the escalating stairwell one step at a time, towards the doors. The doors were tall and towering, and protected her sanctuary, shielding her from the throngs of the nine to five that should be left on the shelf. In each corner of the doorsill sat two cherubs with elbows on knees, keeping tab on the common passersby and warding away as much evil as possible. For every evil vibe they would drop love.

"What a coincidence", I thought to myself. With groceries in my hands and sin on my face, I excitedly smiled at the man briskly jogging the indoor stairwell.

"Hey Glo!" His long fingers and outstretched palms suctioned the glass, thus holding the door.

"Hey Theron", I said to him indirectly. But that feeling soon dwindled to utter submission as his cologne rolled off of him and through my nose like Adie May's Apple Pie fingered me in at one point in time. That aroma would find me while walking back home from school each day at three o' clock. Ms. Adie May would have a pie stinking the whole block up something good. Theron's cologne, though a bit loud on other men, smelled like sexual liberation on him.

"Hey Theron. Where are you headed?" I had to be nosey for you never knew what Theron might be on.

"I'm headed to the grocery store and I was thinking about cooking something decent." "Whatever decent may be", Theron replied with a boyish smile.

With all of the desperation, longing, and penned up sexual frustration that I had ever had in the world, I boldly said, "Well, I'm cooking tonight. Would you like to join me?"

Time froze the moment the last letter rolled off of my tongue. As I longingly waited for the answer, the thickness of anticipation was as deep as the World, waiting to see if the groundhog will see its reflection. Would it be six weeks or six months? The moment encompassed all of this anticipation.

Finally, life rolled off of his tongue as the words "Why not?" came forth.

"Get everything together, and I'll be back around seven. Should I pick up anything?"

Smirking with sweaty palms and obviously blushing, I wanted to tell him to grab some condoms and K-Y, but I merely said, "Don't bring anything except you!"

It was five thirty and I knew not to rush and scramble because to Theron, "around seven" was closer to eight thirty than seven o'clock. I finally got settled into my apartment and I started to clean

86

up. I picked up and empty ice cream container that I left behind over a week ago. I collected all of my underwear that I had left on the bathroom floor. "I am living foul," I scolded myself out loud. I turned on one of my favorite CD's, *The Best of New Birth*, to liven up the cleaning project. I then started to cook and straighten the kitchen as well. "This is ridiculous", I scolded myself again, as I noticed all of the dinner plates stacked in the sink. I vacuumed while mulling over pasta or roast. Theron was the semi-health type, and I knew that roast would be great for a Sunday dinner, but too much for a weekday one. So, I finally decided on lemon-peppered linguine with pesto sauce. I picked out wine from my make shift wine cellar-the pan closet. "Harold Demuiri!" I exalted with a subtle, yet happy jubilation. Theron and I were at the Chambers bookstore on a Saturday hanging out, and ran into a wine tasting function, in which the overzealous wine tasting group insisted that we join them. Every since then, we have been collecting all of the reasonably priced wines from the Southern California vineyards.

"He would really appreciate this red wine," I concluded.

After moments of silence, I cracked open a
window for the breeze to sail through. I sat down
and extracted the Earth from my "mystical
satchel." Breaking the Earth's best as finely as I
could, I took a deep breath of its lingering odor.
To me, it wept like a rainy day in Seattle's lush
hillsides, with a touch of the freshly cut grass in
any inner city park in America. In particular, the
smell was of all the release that I would need for
the evening. Between each thumb and pointer
finger, I gingerly twisted my stresses away and
realized that at that moment it was my *golden time
of day*. Twenty minutes later, nice and relaxed, the
song *Dream Merchant* seemed to pour into the
empty cavities of my mind. I decided to pump the
volume and step into the shower. I normally
copyright a routine of sorts when I am preparing
to get under the water. First, I turn on the water
while adjusting the hot and cold knobs just right.
As the water erupts onto the marble basin, I slyly
peak my toe underneath the *hurt so good*
waterfall. With the right blend of music, water
temperature, and peace of mind, I shed my
clothing like the skin of a shedding serpent. I love
when I can actually feel the water on my face. The
feeling reminds me of an experience or a memory
that I may or may not have ever had or even

known. This was a memory of personal *discovery proportions*, and I felt like I was awakening from a dry muggy slumber, arising to a sound of sensual serenity. Whether that serenity was music or silence, it was a peaceful exhilaration. Maybe I had experienced that emotion sometime ago, or maybe I didn't even have a clue to what it really was. Either way, for almost an hour and a half, I felt that memory and washed my negativities of a long time, away. I got out and dried off, and I then realized that I love being *nice* and in the shower, but doing so for too long sucks as you realize you're a pruned mess of sorts. "Anyway", I said out loud. I rubbed lotion on, feet first then everything else and I began to set the dinner table for two. "Nothing fancy", I assured myself. "Bread basket, candles, place settings, wine glasses, soup plates, dinner plates, pasta bowls, forceps for the pasta, and a snifter for Theron", while itemizing the ambiance. "Every man loves a stiff glass of cognac or scotch after a meal. I learned that from Theron.

Everything was copasetic at this point, so I poured myself a glass of wine and slid into a nice pair of evening pants and a tank top. And like clockwork, I thought, it was eight seventeen, and I heard

Theron walking across the floor upstairs. *Wildflower*, another one of New Birth's finest was blaring from the Nakameche at this point, so I turned it down a bit and sat on the couch waiting. "She's faced the hardest time you could imagine", was the bar that came from the speaker, and a gentle tap sounded above. With every following line, the taps became slower, sensual even. Kind of like a hand gliding and stroking up and down my leg. "Let her cry, for she's a lady," bellowed to the world, and the taps above became louder. Hard, meaningful, stomps continued to pound the floor as if someone was violently kissing me, yet the timbre and intonation of the trail leg reminded me of a hand slowly massaging the naps of my neck, and a voice lovingly coaxing me along. I gingerly placed my glass on the table and the CD stopped. I laid my comfortable soul down, and with the force of clashing bodies, two shoes slammed against the floor above, and I was somehow staring Theron directly into his eyes. His trail leg began to follow his leading leg again, and I could feel the breath of another against my nose, and warming my quivering lips. Suddenly, the evening breeze outside blew in through the window and into my hair. And not only did the bumps around my nipples tighten, but the breeze smelled of truffles, served atop French vanilla ice cream, alongside the still canals of Italy. Awakening from this euphoric paradigm of sorts, I find myself without pants, thus the tapping returned to the metal clank of steel to wood. With my hands pinned to my side, I broke through the barriers to stimulate the creator. The taps got louder and heavier as Theron's trail leg was still gliding across the floor, as I began to moan as I could hear Theron's groans and grunts from his feet tapping the wood. His tapping turned into an orgasmic wail of peak physical ability. Then into a Fourth of July explosion, the trail leg began to beat out the hard kinks of my mental studio floor, and I loved it. And with a leap of silence of sorts followed by a slam, I screamed. The tapping had ended and I would lie there, open to whoever dared to enter. And in the hallway, I could hear the footsteps, *"tap, tap, tap, tap,"* and then a knock at the door. I slowly rose to my feet, still entangled in the euphoria and melody, and satisfyingly opened the door.

"Did you hear it?" Theron asked.

"Yes, Theron, I hear you loud and clear."

"How was it?" he excitedly asked.

I wanted to grab him and take him into the paradigm that I was in. Right then and there and directly in front of the door. Yet instead, I said, "It sounded wonderful."

"Can we eat", he asked. His voice was once again similar to a young boy coming home for dinner after a long day of play.

"Sure!" I replied.

We ate until we both were full of food and conversation, and sitting planted deep into my sofa. From nowhere, Theron leans over and stare me in the eyes. The look he peered traveled directly down into the bowels of my soul's raging water, and down into a ravine where I had only seen and walked in uninhibited.

"Glo, I don't know how to say this," as Theron awakened from his gaze.

He hesitated and glanced towards the floor as if he was a shy love struck teenager, so I said, "What is it Theron?"

"Well, could we dance?" he asked.

And with a smile on my face and Theron's inferno on my mind, I would descend another level.

"Sure Theron", I humbly replied.

"Could you put that New Birth CD on for me Glo?"

Surprised, I said, "Theron, I didn't know you knew of New Birth."

With his boyish charm, he replied, "Neither did I until I danced for you earlier."

The wind outside turned into a quiet storm, and we danced a music never heard in the World before.

The next day, Sum called me at the office.

"Glo?"

"Hey Girl!" I was definitely sounding a little happier than normal.

"Someone is happy", Sum replied as if she could read my mind or sense something different through the phone.

"Not happy," I retorted. "Infatuated, hot, satisfied I am." "Girl!" I would moan, alarming everyone who walked past my open door.

Niedemeyer peeked in, "Are you alright Gloria?"

"Oh yes Joel, just fine."

"Glo! Glo! Glo!" Sum was hollering."

"Girl, it happened", I replied.

"Well, since I don't know what your crazy ass is talking about, what happened? What, you gave somebody head or something. Oh wait a minute, did you get promoted?"

"Sum, only you would think that."

"Girl, you're the crazy one", Sum replied.

"Sum, I finally danced with Theron last night."

And though Sum was on the other line laughing her brains out, and thinking that my job had finally gotten to me, I sat there at my desk performing a pen to desk rendition of Theron's tap.

Story 4:

A Return to Reality

I awoke the next morning, entangled in cotton sheets and sprawled across Glo's floor. I was groggy and my mouth was dry and patchy, and my hands were sticky. We had a wonderful evening, and I must admit that the dancing that I had performed was some of the best tap dancing that I had done in a long while. Maybe the best I have ever performed. Gloria has been obviously listening to my advice. What I expect from a woman that I am involved with, is what she gave. The dinner was a shade above room temperature. Her conversation was educational, humorous, and aloof sometimes, but was ever flowing and she seemed spiritual. After dinner, she even poured me out a warm snifter of cognac. Man oh man!

"Let me head back to my place", I whispered to myself as I pulled my body off of the hardwood floor.

Gloria must have gone to work early. I hope she wasn't late. I know she had a huge proposal to present at work today. I folded her sheet and then tossed it atop of her dry cleaning pile. I gathered my tapping shoes, my pants and my t-shirt. It reeks of her body scent. I slide it on. I then head towards the front door.

Before leaving her place, I bumped into an antique key stand by the door, and to my surprise, there was a note.

"Theron, I enjoyed the wonderful "dancing" we did last night. Let's do dinner later this week. Love, Gloria."

Right there in the door stoop, my mind started to wander. I introspectively rambled on what this woman was thinking. What exactly I had gotten myself into. Not to say that Gloria isn't the type of woman I'd want around. It's just to say…I have no idea what I'm trying to say.

As I walked upstairs, I thought of the days when by happenstance, I would open my curtains before leaving the house. Or maybe it was when I would be coming into the house. Catching Gloria fully engaged in her daily routine. I laughed out loud. I thought to myself that if I were consciously watching this woman, I would be really close to a stalker. Maybe I am a stalker. The thought, though ridiculous, is funny nevertheless.

But seriously, everything happens for a reason. I had a son at twenty-one. Most twenty-one year olds are just beginning to find their definitive voice in the world. The experience was scary, too volatile. It forced me to get to know me on a whole new level. It also gave me strength, courage, and determination. Traits that I never thought I would ever gain in life, let alone in my twenties, including the will to go to graduate school, being with Lindsay and meeting Chloe and marrying her. All experiences ushered me down another trail of self-discovery.

It was after Chloe and the first time in my life that I considered living without my safety net, a higher degree. Never knowing what discoveries lied ahead of my life in a professional environment. I pray that I won't have to ever consider working for the love of money again. Charging in my chips of white-collar life allowed me to help my proverbial mother, sister's, cousins, uncles, and father's. I learned that human rights and Civil Rights were the arenas in which I could serve and make a difference. Black folks in every city that I visited in my lifetime, told me with the same proud yet melancholy gaze. They might need me one day. Maybe they knew that I had eternalized the music of life. Somehow they also knew that I tuned it off for the sake of individualism. Maybe they were just miserable. Their future would be as grim as their body language was expressing the feeling. Regardless of the many stares, I work fifty hours a week, full of slow days, and relatively chill conversations. Taking a moment to catch up with the concerns of those I let fall to the rear view. The legal association I run the books for, and with whom I use as an instrument to give financial advice, provides services to low-income families. Cool gig. I can help people. I can wear my jeans and loafers. I usually have more in common with the people who I help on a day-to-day basis. More than those people I worked with while in the corporate arena.

Being around Lindsay for a short time also enhanced that epiphany. Seeing her in Jamaica, spending several nights of talking and other things last September in Paris, we returned to our separate realities, and we didn't want to move in together. God and his symphony-this life, allowed our paths to cross again. Not to do the inevitable, but to close old ties and to start anew. I can honestly say that Lindsay knew me from the ground up. The real reason that we aren't together is because of our divorces of course. Yet we both knew that we both needed to figure ourselves out.

We were not willing to ruin a good thing for the sake of being comfortable with each other. I will always love Lindsay, for she took the time to think about me as a true to heart friend.

I moved back to the Washington, D.C. area. I live alone. A grown man needs a lot of female attention. Six days out of the week, if possible. Reinventing my dating card, and getting back on the buses of social interaction is never fun, yet always exciting, and assuredly, always a learning process. In Washington, D.C., every black person is or works for an attorney. Every one of the attorneys has a friend who is an entertainer. Everyone drives a car worth more than the condominium that they have just finished purchasing. The same group of attorneys travels extensively, mostly jet setters for a corporate cause and financial gain. From what I learned at the office, those people were intentionally leaving the rest to fend for themselves, more specifically, every Negro for himself. In that vain, there are expansive vacations to Europe, to the Islands, at least three to four times a year. I was slugged by reality, as my game was tired and un-cool for the D.C. scene. In New York, I wore my *big shit on Wall Street* status as a badge. That badge was the courage of my conviction, and my winner's choice. Despite my remodeled brownstone, and decent clothing, in D.C., I am nothing more than an average black Joe. White people know it but dare say it outside of political functions. Black people know it, but won't say it because if they don't have white friends, they feel the same way about themselves. Who wants to be with someone who finds enjoyment in tap dancing? Collecting vinyl records? A guy who is an avid bookworm and homebody? The women in this town seem to party hard and often. One woman told me, "I read enough of the legal briefs that I draft for clients." In retrospect, this is exactly how I wanted my situation to be.

Hence, it was just my luck that I ran across some of the wrong women for me, just a bit different, a bit beautiful and all Black. Never really asking myself why they were wrong. Yet, I would get upset with myself when they blew my mind with their issues and bullshit, including calling when they're not supposed to. Being too busy when its time to call. They made futile attempts to evoke jealously on my behalf. I could care less about her ex-man. I have a few issues, and have harvested them for some time. Every human being deals with issues. Social or life issues are what inherently churn the human complex. And that complex is based upon self-worth. We are as valuable as the pinch of sand that we all are molded from.

I told myself long ago that I couldn't possibly pile on someone else's issues. The mound that I'm dealing with would spill over. She would have to be the epiphany of the air I breathed. More tantalizing than the food I ate. She would be the music I heard from the tapping of steel to wood. In order for me to take on such a responsibility that is, she would be my equal to my better half or greater. She would be a step or two below my mother.

There was Tyna, the postal delivery chick. She passionately made that clear to me the day that we met. I purchased a book of postcard stamps from the post office. She was hard working and hard playing. Hip-hop gear and her lack of moving forward professionally didn't help much. I couldn't deal with her. For Tyna, I could only play some off brand R&B. Monotonous, and outdated, was the energy I received from her. Some days, I was burnt out from her many moods; I would ease her presence by strumming my acoustic guitar. It would be dark with candles, dishes of fruit, cheese and candles spread around my place. She would always start the mood by rushing me. I would quickly acquiesce, eventually laying her down to *You Remind Me*, by R. Kelly. The song is humorous-a man equating a woman to his jeep-but its sweet poetry at its best. Kelly's music is the closest to the Al Green and Otis Redding Rhythm and Blues songs of yesteryear and is perfect for a cartoon like singer, and even fitting for this sweet but complacent and laughable woman.

There was Gina, the massage therapist belly dancer, was a mean massage giver, and would rub me down beyond my shoulders and legs. I could feel her hands behind my heart, and they whispered to me everything would be all right. Gina was a slimmer Billy Holliday and Phyllis Hyman hybrid. She had too many appointments for me to contend with. I only saw her maybe once a week. She would give me a massage, bring some acid jazz through to listen to, and after a half an hour or so of bedroom meandering she would leave with her mask and shallow dress in tow.

There was Flora, a Tax Attorney who practiced here in Washington, D.C. I met her at an art gallery opening in Northwest D.C. near the National Zoo. She was beautiful in all aspects. She was passionate about music-from Bach to Sting. She was five foot four inches, with short curls atop her shoulders, and her torso poured into a snifter. Her legs calmly played the role of the short stem. Her feet were soft and well manicured, and the base of the stem fittingly held her brown cognac. You could see that it was half full yet half empty and Flora's body fingered in all men. I, the fool of the bunch, made the proverbial call. She was the perfect drink. Her walk would shift side-to-side, enticing the youngest fools and playing fiddle with the wisest owls. Flora was the finest cognac that your soul could buy. The intoxicant, brown and amber- the perfect color for a cognac-smelled and gave the heaviest high. She lacked the main ingredient of the drink

Soul or flavor, whatever you call it, can be best described as that pocket in a beat that forces your body to move to its rhythm. Its hollow and forceful heartbeat places your ultimate vibe against the backdrop of that perfect setting sun. That World surrounded by the bluest water was pure, with waves and colors as detailed as a picture of sweet paradise.

How could a woman who never faced difficult times, deal with a man who was churned from hard times? That man who is given a hard time on a daily basis? The soul that a burden carrying man needs for comfort and one that he could consider a mate. She should provide him solace when the world is kicking him in the ass. Not even one of his best friends can help ease that stress, for only that soulful woman can comfort him. That woman will rub your aching back, kiss your pressured temples, and wash the head of your stressed out mind of clutter and crap. Dependent upon your actions, she might give you that ultimate dream. More importantly, she will leave you on your back, looking to the sky, thanking your one and only God. You love her and adore her beyond the superficial or sexual things that you loved every other woman before her. Everything that she does is out of pure kindness and understanding, and that type of epiphany can come from any one woman, devoid of hard times. Past experiences, including my marriage, would suggest otherwise. That is the truth for me and for other black men, maybe or maybe not churned from the same past as I am. This truth isn't a truth but an enduring fallacy. Everyone has a particular drink to drink. Who am I to knock another man's hustle? In my case, it would be like the pot calling the kettle black. Some people still crown me a sellout and an Uncle Tom. Never will those people know or understand my plight.

Any drink of cognac can have a sweet smell, a wonderful body, and presented to you warmed and cozy with a Punch cigar. John Coltrane can keep the background pleasant anywhere, even in Mississippi or Montreal. He has played there himself before. Will that drink that you take, do what's needed to be done to your soul? My grandfather, in a slurred dialect, told me that, "any alcohol that you drink is bad for you. But in this life, you'll find that you very well may become dependent on a drink every now and then. Drink that spirit which will help to ease the stresses. Quell the burning issues that you're dealing with." Right before he told me this, he was making a joke with my great uncles about women. A woman has been the downfall of a many great men. I love women so much. Why would I settle for a woman who couldn't get me to that ultimate high? Flora and I stopped talking. We run into each other. Each time I see her shimmy and her smile, I wonder what if? She is a tax attorney in Washington, D.C. I see her with a lot more black men then I once did. She knows that there are conscientious and equal leveled-financially and socially- black men out there for her. Maybe I was brought into her life to show her that. Despite appearances, the majority of black men in D.C. aren't rogues, hustlers, and homosexuals. Popular culture in D.C. will suggest otherwise. Stereotypes that rip at the fear of any people can be used maliciously. This is the popular culture that most of us have come to adore.

I sometimes force the issue with finding a good woman. I go to places where I knew I could find at least one woman to proposition. Some days, I take the faithful art gallery trek. I visit art museums and photo shops searching for something. Each time, I run into the queasy thoughts of my ex-wife Chloe and Flora even. My vibe would be off at that point. Rather than taint my aura, I stopped that trek for a while. I tried the *nature-Zen trek*, in which I force fed myself granola and health nuts for a month while hiking in Rock Creek Park. A dry month it was as I also took some yoga classes, searching for the natural and bohemian cuties. Yoga in itself is a decent avenue for release. The classes are saturated with women going through a lot of personal stresses-those with work or relationships. An avenue of swapping some release and support energy from other women. The few men that were in those sessions were either getting in touch with their feminine side, or those who were clever like me, and wanted an easy path to finding a decent woman.

It's easier dealing with a woman that I have never spoken with and met at a bar, than those women who I have known and found out things about, for some reason. Having a fresh female personality around is exciting. I have yet to find a woman that I could keep around. One who keeps things fresh each time we see each other, and maintains her own individuality. When I did find her, she was right under my nose-literally.

Gloria and I were converging on a real intimate level, without realizing it. At first, we were strictly friends who made gentle calls to remind one another to take out the trash or to get some new music. We offered one another advice on people we were dating, and spoke to each other about other mutual interests that any other woman and man would share. We would sip wine at wine tasting events. Pick food to cook for dinner. We had that uncomfortable feeling around other people. That one feeling as a little boy that made you blush and in turn, hit your best friend for telling the girl you had a crush on, that you indeed had a crush on her. Sort of like passing gas in a crowded room and someone pointing it out to everyone that it was you who passed gas. That's the feeling. Our families and friends always highlighted the fact of how wonderful a couple we would make. Our relationship always seemed to be much greater than being close friends. The biggest question about Gloria was, "could she give me the inspiration that I needed from a woman?" I always felt that she couldn't. I swore that I knew her type of woman.

Gloria works ridiculous hours because she has no other outlets and needs the money. Her meticulous manicured façade and wardrobe told the World something differently. From that picture, I deduced that she was very conservative in the bedroom and selfish-all about her spot. It seems as if you couldn't pay her to service you. She juts looks unaccommodating, dry, and dare I say

uneventful. Fireman often realized the same thing
when they pulled a family out of a burning house.
Despite the fact that the house is burning down,
and at any second the roof might fall in, someone
is going to risk the whole thing reaching for their
photo album. And if the album is not retrieved,
after the fire has been quelled, the Fireman isn't
thanked but is chastised. And like them, I would
think of shooting Glo dead in the mouth with my
water hose too. I thought that maybe she listened
to any popular music that came on the radio. Too
busy to catch a review in Mojo or maybe even
Billboard Magazine and never purchased new
music. She always looks stunning. Stopping past
my house to request my approval, gliding her five
foot nine inch frame (five foot ten with heals) out
of the house for a girl's night out. Her friends
Summer (a crazy fool) and Li (A sexy yet stumpy
Asian woman) always revealed to me that it was
something Gloria wasn't saying to me. Her one
hundred and thirty pound mass was creasing at the
bottom back of her evening jackets. The music
that she played each morning was familiar to me
for some reason. I could barely hear the music.
She was considerate enough not to blast it too
loud. Bessie Smith, the Anthology, offered a tune
or two that I needed to hear right at that moment.

Somewhere around those thoughts is where I realized that what I had been looking for was right in my face, and a snake would have assuredly bitten me right on the nose.

And without words, I would run into Gloria at the grocery store more often, or while having filmed processed, more frequently.

"Eventually", I conceded to myself, "when the time is right and the stars are aligned enough to see the Achilles, I will approach Gloria on another level."

Knowing what Gloria liked about men, and she knowing what I liked about women, we manipulated our collective vibe with subtle hints and deep stares of longing and adornment. Rather than grazing hands, we would find ourselves clutching hands. We'd glance over when we felt one another's heartbeat and release each others hand. We would smile shortly thereafter. Not showing the other too much.

"Dinner was no fluke", I thought out loud. Replacing the bolt on my antique Victrola, I put a record on to play and the arm falls off. My hands either write, or restore any of the antiques that I have around the house. It eases my mind and gives me serenity. Allows me to be the doctor I always wanted to be. I can't get my mind off of Gloria.

"Now what though?"

"Never should I have let this woman into my cipher."

"Convenience or otherwise, the note she wrote speaks volumes about her personality."

At that point I figured that I was being way too cynical, maybe overly analytical.

"Damn you Theron." "Damn you", as I boyishly whispered to myself in the mirror.

As I laced up my tapping shoes and looked out the window, I watched as the day was headed towards dusk. It was if someone was slowly dozing off to chill sonatas, or the hum of blues musician, \and when the music stops the person falls asleep into a pensive and internal celebration. It was time to vent my daily stresses. My day off from the Green

Mill was consumed on an antique that still doesn't work properly and this woman.

"I can't lie to myself", I thought. "Gloria and I made sweet music last night."

"Let's do dinner later this week", I once again whispered aloud and laughed a bit.

"The nerve of that broad", I thought.

I started to tap with no music, except for that which was thumping through my chest.

Twenty minutes into my session, there was a knock at the door.

"Good I thought", Lindsay, told me that she was sending a couple of new records to me.

"Maybe these are it."

I jogged to the door, almost falling over my tap shoe.

I was surprised to see Gloria standing there in a tight black dress and tapping shoes.

Her beautiful eyelashes were batting at me as if I was her daddy. She had been naughty. She blushed. Her skin glistened from the evening sun. Blondish brown short curls were pulled back with a black and white printed scarf. I envisioned her hand touching my face, and thought of how her feet would graze my left cheek.

With the sternest voice that I knew and usually stared at Sun when he was out of place, I paused for a second.

"What are you doing home from work so soon?"

"I took off the rest of the day after my presentation."

"Oh, okay, what's going on with you?" I said this nonchalantly as if I didn't already know.

She must have known that I was a little upset at her note.

And with a cool and cheerful demeanor she started to sing her own version of love.

We laughed.

She tilted her beautiful head towards me, a sweet offering for a now eventful day. I leaned over her with a kiss on the forehead.

"So, we'll have dinner next week huh?" I sarcastically said to her. She attempted to take a step forward into my house. I acquiesced to her body language.

We both started laughing, and the tapping lessons began.

Reality Check:
The Distant Now

Sitting alone at a New Years Eve party in SoHo, Manhattan my mind started to wander to a time when I thought that I would never have the opportunity to be *the man*. For some reason, I witnessed myself in the context of the future, sitting on the curb watching aged friends walk by. I could only sit and watch because I was old, but looked young, and for someone reason, young children weren't allowed to cross the street alone. The only way I could make it across was if a dame took my hand and coaxed me along. It was a weird inner vision for what it's all worth, but definitely a telling tale of fear and anxiety so my palms now describe through these keys.

I can recall junior high school. I believed that there could be nothing better than playing basketball in the thunder and lightning. The rain would tighten the curls on my already nappy head. The basketball had to be gripped just a bit more. The shot could squeak through the wet basketball nets, with the sideline cameras clicking and flashing. It was childish innocence. Around the same time, I would have a baseball game before noon, a summer basketball game at 4:00 p.m., an obligation to meet friends at the outside public basketball court to play with the old heads, shortly thereafter.

This was at the same time that reality forced my closest friends and me to gauge where we would be ten years from that very moment. Retrospectively, moments like this only came when we played basketball with the older dudes. These guys were once above average in basketball, had the newest sneakers; Converse, with color laces. Their designer jeans were tailored and they wore their collars aloof. They attended the one public high school that we would be going to. Some were distant relatives. Family members detached by nothing more than the different city blocks that we all lived on. All were in their late thirties and stuck in their childhood neighborhood, working odd jobs, while aimlessly roaming the streets in their free time. Maybe they wanted to be there. The advice they would give us forced us to realize otherwise. All of us young guys had grand ideas about the future. We talked about the cars we would have, the parties that we would attend, and the women that we would take home. Honestly assuming that we would one day be professional athletes, having the luxury of taking whatever woman we wanted home. For some reason, this was the only avenue we knew of. Drug dealers were cool, but they encompass the same group of complacent few that we refused to become. Somehow, amongst all of the talking, we would pause on the bench and hear the wind whisper soft-spoken words and promises of things to come. Even then, I couldn't lie to myself. I knew that I was an above average basketball player. Not physically talented and without the right system intact. There was no way that I could market myself to the big time colleges. My calling was well beyond the basketball courts and sports on a whole.

At this loft party in SoHo, ten years later, a soft-spoken breeze told me that, "all that is here before you, is what I have to offer YOU. All of the grand ideas, the grand revelations, and the boasting and bragging, are far from the ideas that you had. Though you didn't ask for this experience, it was given to you. What do you plan to do with this experience?" I snapped out of my momentary trance, standing middle ground, in a room full of people. It was if I was a bottle top with a tapestry of colors and experiences that I could only imagine, painted inside of me, and when the spin was done, I stopped to only find that that tapestry was blank siding, and what I had written and seen was an oasis, and held nothing of relevance to my reality. These people were entangled in their individual paradigm, trying desperately to find release and momentary freedom. They were using everything in the moment to rise a bit higher. Luxury was free. The reality was nothing they had anticipated. And whether they were on a basketball court, or a yacht, you somehow knew; life had whispered to them as well. They exalted the past year, the past decade. Their childhood was raised for sacrifice to the ghosts of things to come, while enjoying one another for that moment. I was being too analytical at the time as me eyes possessed such a look because of the marijuana being passed around. I am no different from the next man. My perceptions are just as wrong as others. I was mentally ignited and metaphysically shot out of this world when I realized; the future is absolutely nothing until it happens and comes to pass. Gross assumptions that we indulge in as children are planted and nurtured by other and taken into adulthood. We are left blind to the reality that we actually embark upon when life or possibly death makes its rounds. The future I was in would be awesome to others, and that future was not only a surprise,

That Future was and is an everlasting awakening to the realm of what is.

To all of those who read this and can relate in any way, I didn't party that night. I just sat there and allowed my soul to digest this new scene. Friends whizzed by as the spirits of the evening kept my paradigm whirling through the night, but inside, my World was as steady as the hand on a cuckoos clock, with the cuckoo and I looking eye to eye and asking one another, "who's really cuckoo?" Not a minute sooner or later, I realized that the not so distant future that I was excited about as an adolescent was now my reality. Whether I wanted to party or not, drink or not, smoke or not, or *spit some game at some dame*, the experience would come and go, twinkling in the skies of my memories like the same childish thoughts that I internalized at twelve, and that were left to become false by those who told me that in a free country, anything is possible. My not so distant future was a flash and a future that would just as quickly be my past. This is the second reality check. Reality, like reality does, checked me directly into the cheap seats where I belong. I just sat there, devoid of pride, and listened, learned, and planned.

Story 5:

The Alternative Psychoanalysis

It was his fourth and last year working for the Department of Corrections. Chauncey "Chuck" Norwood was hired straight from the night program at the University of the District Columbia with a degree in Social Psychology. While working as a Dependency Officer for two years, the Warden asked him to take over the vacant Alternative Psychological program. He happily accepted the position, while finishing up his Master's Degree through the night program at John Hopkins University. His degree was in Rehabilitative Psychology. This was the program he sincerely believed that would garner him the professional recognition that he always wanted. He was Chuck or Elijah to the inmates, for he would get those not sure of themselves, sure of their own stature as men, and was talented enough to deliver a message to each individual man who came through his program. But he never thought that he would get a lesson. And the main reason he was leaving his post was because of the fact that what he learned a few years prior from one of his best patient, was the truth and had and would never be changed. He recalls his stroll around the room, he remembers his chest being puffed out, and how coolly he stared around the room at the men who he hoped at the time, got something out

124

of his program. He can still see the many glances around him, but it was the look down at his notebook that he remembers perfectly. He remembers the names vividly and remembers how each name told a story of what everyone had gone through in their life, and what they would return to when they left. Some were headed to Austin, Texas; those boys had been in the system all their life, and because of budget cutbacks, could no longer be held in Virginia. The others were tossed to the doorsteps of society with thirty dollars, and nothing more than what they walked into the door with. Oftentimes, that was the clothes they had on their back, a wallet with no money, and their new air of freedom. He remembers slapping hands with a couple of guys but he remembers meeting Earl for the first time. He can't recall whether he connected eyes with him; Earl was always the low-key type, and smarter than everybody thought. But the conversation was priceless.

Chuck remembers the conversation that he shared with Earl amongst the fray of the freed pigeons.

"I plan on posting your paper "The First Thing You'll Do When You Get Out". "It was an inspiration."

"Chuck, I won't be back here again. And that's not because I am reformed, or because I have participated in your class. I won't be back here again, because I didn't do anything in the first place; I am merely a Blackman trying to survive. I am considered an animal, and I was placed in an environment and caged like an animal, and they expect me to be reformed after caging me?"

Chuck remembers standing in ah, and staring out into an empty room. He was baffled because Earl had never shown any rebellion towards the group or the anointed Elijah. But he remembers being interested in what Earl had to say.

"Chuck, do you even know why they put me in here?"

Chuck remembers staring off, and realizing that he did not actually know why Earl had been confined to jail. He just remembers himself falling into one of his chairs, and he becoming the person in need of therapy.

"No Earl, I don't know why they put you in here."

"I am the least of your worries. I won't be back here because I never wanted to be here in the first place. I was forced here, for a crime that's not even recognized as a crime in the Jungle."

"But from what I observed from your classes, and life in this place, the people that are here are happy to be here. And the reason why they're happy is because just like any animal on the streets, scratching to get the minimum, by any means necessary, you are merely confirming the fact that one is an animal, and putting them in an environment to do just that without any major consequences. How are we punishing someone by taking away their freedom, when they actually never felt free in the first place?"

"Chuck, the issues run much deeper than you think. Imagine Chuck for one minute. Imagine not having a mother or father, and at twelve years old trying to figure out how you're going to eat, in a World, and more specifically a country, where you have to have money to walk in some neighborhoods. Food has to come from somewhere, and as far as I know, you need at least a GED to work at a fast food joint"

"Imagine chuck. Can you imagine not eating, and not knowing where your parents are? Can you imagine succumbing to not having money in a country that runs exclusively on money? Can you imagine being ridiculed and ignored just because you don't have money and your clothing shows it?"

Chuck stares away, with his hands in his lap.

"Chuck, the majority of the people in here already feel like an animal, displaced in a jungle where survival goes the fittest. You put them in a cage, and they learn to think differently, and act differently and they become bitter and hateful. It's the same language they speak through eye contact on the streets. There are weaklings outside these walls. In here, there are beasts against beasts. There are rules to their society of survival that is different from your reality and even mine. They test one another's fears, they challenge a man's manhood with gestures, and they force you to shit or get off of the pot, everyday. They don't love living this way; it's all that they know-it becomes natural at certain points. And I really can't say they, as if I am not a part of those that I speak of. My mentality is no different and my rage is specific in its direction, as I choose to challenge other systems using different tactics. In the end, we all end up where our energy's are directed."

"Chuck, do you realize that out of the men who are chosen for your program, the majority of them will not come back. And not because they are reformed, but because they played the jungle for what it's worth and scratched their way into your program? They acted the role given to them to get here. Chuck, they won't be back because they'll either take heed or die. Chuck, you are the gatekeeper to the outside. In the jungle, you are the being that lets the lions out of the forest and into the gazelle coup. They adapt to what you need to get them out, and they follow it, and offer you what you need to hear to get them out. With that said Chuck, your program is nothing but a way to help folks get through their issues. Issues that are so deeply rooted, that the only ways that they will ever let them go are because either A, God intervenes, or B, they succumb to the jungle. Not because they write a story, or learn to think as a sane person prepared with the tools of functional and sane people. Deprivation coupled with hopelessness will drive any human being insane."

"Chuck, it's been real. Some of us play a game and some of us are used as pawns in a game played by others. My friend, I'm glad that you are so naïve, and in this place, and like America, you will always be that pawn. No one wants your job because they would be held accountable for actually rehabilitating a grown man. The people who need to be rehabilitated love you because not only do you give them an angle to consider, but you provide them with something they've never had in life; someone who gives a damn. And for that, they owe you something. That's a creed that every person has, but is a creed that people of the jungle, and who are consumed by the streets, live by. In here, you're a pawn in the jungle. And regardless of how hard you try, it's the man that stops the madness. Not the environment, but the man. And that man doesn't start being a man at eighteen, but it starts the day he is snatched out of that warm and dark apartment that afforded him free food, free rent, and unlimited attention for nine months. Maybe you should actually use that paper up there on the wall and start with the youth. If you don't get them then, don't expect to get them now. Free will is a catch twenty-two, dependent upon which side of the power you reside on."

Earl stands and extends his hand. Chuck looks up at Earl and extends his. As Earl walks out, he turns and stops.

"Chuck, you helped me to understand myself on many different levels. I am happy that I'm leaving, but sort of sad. Happy because I have little time from now on to think about my circumstances as a free man. I'm sad because I will never have the opportunity to see life in its essence. To see human nature, as it would be if none of this shit we use as crutches was a part of the World. I'm also sad, because I can't get anymore of these free sessions to get myself together."

Chuck smiles.

"Chuck, do you have a cigarette?"

<u>Earl's Story</u>

"I awoke in the blackness. Fully
awake now, I simply lay there as though
paralyzed. I could think of nothing else to do
Later I would try to find my way out, but I could
Only lie on the floor, reliving the dream."

As the invisible man in Ralph Ellison's tale "The Invisible Man", it seemed that while soul searching and somehow paralyzed, I stumbled into a descent through an abyss. Falling, frantically grasping at the walls around me, catching each root and stone edge in the back and face, I broke through my soul's dormant state of paralyses. Finding in the dark, exactly what I had endured over a lifetime in a mere thought of a bright flickering, smoky light. Unconsciously, within my euphoric grandeur, I likened my life to a cigarette. Not a particular brand. To the many that experience life, there is a brand that they crave and a brand that they live. Devoid of the brand they prefer, they will smoke until their hearts content. Enjoy the nicotine and tar that lies between the lines. Whether that tar and nicotine is light or with or without menthol, it is still a cigarette nevertheless. A cigarette will burn whether you inhale, puff or merely light it. The smoke it emits hits every smoker's soul differently. Performing whatever duties it may throughout the human anatomy. Simultaneously, the fume from the cigarette conquers the craving beast and he seems insurmountable. The bastard appears to be two stories tall, an infinite amount of pounds, and has the mind control mechanism of the first human being who truly captivated you, and knew that they were doing it. You metaphysically mutate into a one armed pious gimp, attempting to slay a giant freak of full composure with a broken pebble. Faith alone may help you. Prayer becomes your own security. Self-Esteem becomes an oxy moron. In between the puffs, a cigarette will inherently attract other elements to its cipher. Personal surroundings become social surroundings. The attracted might be a drink of any kind or some food, and maybe conversation. You can't hide nor run. It's connected to you beyond the obvious. You're intrigued and fascinated by its glory. Meanwhile, its paper continues to burn and you feel a sense of abandonment, and hence pull and puff. Only a few puffs are used to pacify the craving beast. Everything between the papers is toxic, and encourages us to smoke over and over and over again. We attempt to slay the giant. The fight is fruitless. We can't possibly stand in with the impossible and throw our dwindling souls into the wind. We are slowly and meticulously killing all of the righteous organs in our bodies while perpetuating a cycle that is nothing short of sheer hopelessness.

It is difficult to realize that my life is like a cigarette, and all of the realities that surround one. I have been back home from well, that's my business, but to the City, if you must know. It's where I am. Atop the trash and jungle floor, riding atop the smog and displaced wails of social infidelity. Whichever substantially sized city you should choose on God's great Earth, I am there. Please use your imagination. Be cognizant that I am around. You have seen me. I am as common as the spent, wet filters you may ignore while running through your own paradigm. You don't recognize me because I blend in just as well. Amongst the many brands of lifestyles, living situations, and instances, there, you can see, and have seen Ole' Earl. And like no other, I get my fix of nicotine. The giant it is. I have always been familiar with the city. I was uprooted in and around it. I walk city, talk and study the city. From time to time I suppose that I inherently need the City. I don't know it as much as it doesn't know me or Vice versa. Or maybe for an instant, it doesn't care to know or understand me. I foolishly leap into the depths of the city. Without a conservative abandonment, I plunge into the not so clairvoyant brooks of reality. With my invisible fortune in tow, I desperately search and seek, while subconsciously waiting to be snatched back up by my metaphysical bungee cord.

Hopping On the Train to Work

Never fulfilled by riding the trains, rather the distaste is because of cold stares or the reality impaired, I refuse to believe that everything is horrible. I allude to church and how time flies by when you are at peace. It is that time when the only beast that becomes an issue is the momentary growl of hunger-mentally or physically. I mentally sing as I reflect on my many strolls to the office. My stroll is similar to a floating glide of disbelief. I am pinned to this floating glide, reality consisting of sitting behind a desk for eight hours, accepting the hypnotic intoxicants of capitalism, which technically is the proverbial bait, the "mighty dollar". A light head I have, with a mind full of overcast haze. A stroll regulated by a time unseen and a dollar unearned. This glide is a walk that you must take everyday. Unless. Do you want to be the faceless butts that you step over daily? Do you want to be those same anomalies that you stingily offer pennies on the dollar? Those that you Pacify with pity and use to pamper your own self-esteem? Through my day at the office, I take several smoke breaks to crack the monotony of my quiet and un-stimulated mind. Feigning to pucker and pull I would hit the side door to avoid the cold stares and sullen smiles. A quick hello would suffice. Yet, I understood that everyone in that same office was searching for something three times as hard as I. From the many conversations that I had with those dedicated employees, some searched for the money to take that next vacation. Some were searching for enough money to find that next rush of adrenaline through an expensive bottle of Scotch, or at the bitten end of a vintage cigar-whichever offered the best escape. Some of those people searched for meaning. Any meaning to any of their daily routines would help. They wondered whether they should go this way or that way; HMO or PPO, Democrat or Republican, Socialist or Communist, long term or short term bonds, Bear or Bull, or evil or more evil. Some just searched to make ends meet. Enough leverage to pay the bills, and to drive freely, with maybe enough economical force left over to provide for their children another reason to smile. They relished the time and patience to tinker with a prized possession-a thirty-year-old record player. Technology always has a way of distorting the true message. Those were the people whom I loved most. They smoked the same cigarette as I. They loved me and would love me, whether I was homeless or heathen. God touched them differently. He allowed them to respect everyone equally, and to not be the subjective or objective human being-not to be that one group of people whom gauge character by deducing from skin tone, clothing worn, and family history. They are solid. The people I speak of are the people whom hate to see another human being succumbing to the jungle. While in my corner of the smoker's lounge, I inhaled whichever type of cigarette that the players might offer a butt. Whatever cigarette and brand of people that was around to fulfill my human desires and insecurities. I began to understand the politics of the smoker. Newport's or Marlboro Lights seldom were seen in the same circles of conversations. Any of the brands outside of the two were body-less in ashtrays and relegated to a totally different smoker's lounge. The city has unwritten rules, which are similar to those unwritten about all of us smoking together in the first place. I likened this attitude to a common theme of denying someone else happiness, on the basis that we all are unhappy. I constantly asked myself why I fell into the games that these people play. Why did I conform to the vices that lured me down the desolate hallways of social suicide? As many weekends as I could remember, I would commute on a train to get to the city of smokers.

The Weekend

I would hang with smoking friends, joined without an ample degree of separation. Not together as in the same pack of cigs, but together by relationship. I would tag along, fully unable to attract that decent woman who could entertain me, and I her, while in the company of this social group. To this day, I believed that no female appreciated me. I didn't conform to the media perceptions of black men in pop culture. I smoke and listen to Coltrane because he and his modal brethren are the only musical beings that I can truly understand. Miles entrances me and keeps me on a fantastic high. Shows me how the Spaniards are. I read. Apparently, Black Americans do not. Why separate myself? Newspapers, magazines, or general chapbooks are diamonds and rare stones, as gems are hidden in the midst of most work that comes across ones path. I guess now we don't like gems. Everything's tangential when the crap is all cleared and is filler for a life story yet to fully unfold. But how alias I must have looked to the World and more specifically, this group of people, as a mere accessory? I was just a smoker at this point, dying of a thirst for more from this life, and stomach bulging due to hunger or more closely to home, a change in seasons. I was longing for a shift in patience while traveling across the airs of nothing, blaming the World for my action or lack thereof. Smoking on whatever type of cigarette I had of my own. I found myself burning off of those whom at least found out where they were and more importantly who they were. And because I could not face the sight or truth of myself, I became a cigarette. I couldn't imagine stepping outside of myself, gazing behind two other people whom truly found themselves through one another. But when I did venture out of self, I became something of an entertainment prop or an accessory to the reality. In loneliness, I felt the strain of the pull. One of the persons would aimlessly find comfort in my rich taste. In anxiety, times of being around other unknown people, I would be the time passed until the rest of the group would waltz in. Only to be mashed out at the height of my final flicker. My search became an arena to hoist jokes and pathetic gestures of humility. Thanks. Not in the physical, but in the metaphysical. I was in their hands, burning and smoking. And I realized it all, because though I was now an ordained cigarette, I craved as a smoker to return to their comfort time and time again. And return I did. Not exactly knowing why I had bothered in the first place. In being lost and without companionship, a brand of my own, I latched onto others who did have those things, bumming off of their emotions and experiences as if those experiences were my own. I did this, possibly against those people's true aspirations and feelings, and because I further needed those feelings and unwarranted emotions, the gimp tried his luck with the dice again. He crapped out. I became a nicotine addict. Even when I wasn't puffing my own cigarettes and bumming for my own cause, I was being the very thing that I dreaded; a cigarette. I lacked so much in my life, yet I had so much to give. Modal, avant-garde, bebop, nor hip-hop could get me out of my stupor. People from every social circle gravitated towards my aura. Asking could I spare something. They needed to get by too, even though they were too poor to cope. Far worse than a cigarette, as they were narcotics recovering, somehow realizing that a human cigarette could defer the time. I had no idea what they wanted. The attraction that my brown ivories fingered in couldn't have been that significant to warrant a conversation. Ole' Earl must have been fooled and brainwashed into thinking he had nothing left.

My Psyche

I was a glorious un-smoked cigarette to some. No one dared to touch an off brand. For weeks, I would continue to bum off of my social friends. Used to my capacities as a cigarette. Alone, the seasons no longer had definitive meanings to me. I coasted through reality, with my own cigarette in tow; chain-smoking and light headed, until they were all gone. At that point, I realized that when you reduce yourself in any way to creating a substitution, you ultimately become your substitution. Anything emotionally that you are substituting because of your own lack thereof, you will gravitate towards. Your cycle will once again become an addiction. In finding fulfillment, other people will use your personal relations because they are searching just as hard. Personally, I cannot comprehend why I transformed into such an entity, but I did. I was and still am an off brand.

The Aftermath

My train completed its last trip from the city to the dead-burbs, and from there I decided to walk. But before I would think of anything else, I felt the snap of the bungee. Through the abyss I landed firmly on my feet, understanding the gist of my reality.

"So there you have all that's important.
Or at least you almost have it-or showed me- the
hole I was in, if you will- and I reluctantly
accepted the fact. What else could I have done?
Once you get used to it, reality is as irresistible as
a club, and I was clubbed onto the cellar before I
caught the hint."-Epilogue, "The Invisible Man",
by Ralph Ellison

Chuck packs up his desk and grabs his plaques off of the wall. He accepted a gig working with troubled youth in Northeast Washington D.C. He should've done it sooner. Resign and all, and actually do something meaningful. He reminisces over that conversation, and unfolds the paper that Earl wrote one week before he was to be on his way out of the door. He smiles. He smiles. He then thinks that his therapy actually didn't help a single soul. It only prolonged a process of the lost that eventually have to take accountability and find themselves.

Story 6

Blue Legato:

A Child's Religion

I know this evening to be a late hazy night, as the sky is dark, with streaks of gray. It is humid. The lead walls are crying. The fan's screen has collected dust, mosquitos, and the words of dead men walking. I anxiously realize that traffic is running in and out the front and back doors-a slam here, a crash there, a kick and scratch there. This exchange of people is similar to a busy intersection. Neither side streets-nor closets, nor locked and closed doors are retreats from the cringing hustle of the hustling World's beat. A screen door plays the stoplight, and in trying to watch television I stand at the corner waiting for the white walking man up and over yonder.

"Please flash!" Grant me clearance and deliverance to the other side. And as sure as he blinks, is enough to know that I will cross the street. I don't think twice that he will not show his presence, though we mostly live by faith and not by sight. Sometimes it's better to see some change. I know he will show himself. Similar to a train depot, some of the long and dark faces are known. Some of the people are short, or light skinned ones, with balled heads and tan skin. Some had pale and tar black skins. Others, you just understood their plight. Everyone needs to get from point A to point B, regardless if they are steaming through to find that picker upper. Somehow they do not know that the real picker upper comes from within. Deep down sunny pastures offers the rays of hope, and altering ones reality can never attain what those people search for. They rely on an undue fallacy. Physical abuse and the mental stimulation of drug abuse can bring them closer to Zen. I am not mad though, not at those who use nor those who use others to use. I am merely concerned about the traffic. You learn fast from those you look up to, nodding to a blues and jazz that goes unheard. They're somewhere else, beyond my understanding. Leaving but a corpse to admire and study the biology of a dying breed. Big hands and strategic marks on arms are like trains as well. Running noses mimic blown smoke stacks and signifies a need to recharge. They are whispering, to anyone who dares to listen. A train is a coming through. Sure, I am not yet naïve. Fighting against what is wrong, though I am young enough to know that what I marvel at and live within is not right, Right? What is really right or wrong? A World where you know of no one catching a break? Death from Diabetes, Cancer, strokes, and heart attacks have become the trivial norm. Just as dawn turns to dusk, another family member turns over in their grave to welcome the next defaulted soul. You realize that you are a product of a clan infatuated with the escapism of death's fury. It's in my music, my clothes, and my haircut. It's violent, unforgiving and unremorseful. And who am I, but a nappy headed product of a project situation, thinking freely while accepting projections of failure because of my pedigree. How can you possibly succeed when you are afforded and force fed failure from day one? If there is such a thing as a race, you run it from day one with no leg below the knees. In order to compete, you find any means to get the necessary prosthesis. At least give me a chance to walk, let alone run. Even gaining one percent of a fighting chance is fuel enough to carry on. Just a quarter tank of fuel, a quart of oil, and a battery, will keep a car moving. From the moment of conception, and as competition becomes your mantra; you know that winning will never be an option. From that moment of clarity, you feel uncomfortable amongst white people. You then find truth by whispering to your inner-self, Black people from a functional pedigree also hate me. Amongst the entire fray, I find inner visions to remain me. Nappy hair, knotty head, fit full of heathen tendencies and inner infidelities, coupled with Worldly iniquity, feeling half dead at the tender age of nine…ten…eleven…twelve…and thirteen. Where will my future be? My lips move in unison with the reflection that peers back at me. For many days and nights, I search aimlessly for any type of prophecies. At thirteen, I scream alone, wearily strolling through a paradigm alone. I am learning to fend for my tiny self-alone. May God grant me clearance to stay myself a home of my own, may God grant me clearance to stay myself a home of my own. Where will I be tomorrow? I hope and pray that tomorrow will be.

Story 7:

A New Generation of Jive

(Learned Actions)

"What's up young?" Stumbles and Sticks shouted in unison as Black crossed the street wearing timberland boots, drop aerobic socks, jean shorts, a white wife beater and a tilted Polo cap. It's all coupled with a speck of innocence and a hint of arrogance. He might fuck you up.

"Aint shit" Black replied. "Hot as a mother fucker out this joint." "Ya'll niggers got anything to drink?" Black stated, with a smug smirk on his face.

Jamis Wallace aka Black- nicknamed because his skin is as dark as the rundown end of a lead pencil. Richard Lawson aka Stumbles- nicknamed because he had a speech impediment, in which he skipped words when he spoke. Lyle Stubblefield aka Sticks- nicknamed because he was skinnier that than a stick, so it seemed, two maternal cousins and a cousin-a person whom you adopt as your cousin, and your family. He's not your real kin. If circumstances were different you would choose that man as your cousin, a brother. The three hung out on the corner of whatever street that is "hot", both in heat and "high action." This was a summer evening, anywhere in America.)

"Nah nigga, you black ass, hot foot having ass nigga. Always want something to drink." Stumbles blurts out the joke in Black's direction while waving definitive gestures. He might fuck you up as well.

"Ah, I know you aint joning nigga (cracking a joke). With that bama ass Bo Jackson T-shirt you got on." Replies Black, as everybody laughs in unison.

"And you Sticks ass nigga. Yo head look like a fucking hook." The boy's laughter could be heard louder, and echoed against the brick row house walls.

"Stumbles, that's your mother aint it?" Sticks asks the two other boys with a stern pointer finger gesture, and in a tone only used by the boys when a situation warranted serious attention. He was passive and always aloof, and always knowing something greater than the others. Innocence was long gone. He won't fuck you up physically. Something in his mannerisms frightens you.

"Damn, she back from the grocery store already."
Stumbles reply, with a hint of concern in his
voice.
"I know she brought back something to drink",
Black blurts out with another smug smirk on his
face.

"Ah, you black as nigga." Stumbles Replies.

"Drink some water", Sticks screams into Black's
ear as they start to laugh.

"There you go", says black, while standing with
his hand on his chin and staring down Sticks with
a sarcastic look.

"Nigga, you need to grow some hair over them
knots on your head." The three dudes split from
the center of conversation, and one falls on the
ground, one falls on the fence and one falls atop
the hood of the car, all clutching their stomachs
with laughter pains.

"Nah for real you dumb ass football face niggas."
"I'm about to roll to my grandma's house for the
weekend to cool out." "The central air really is
"on point" when it's this hot out this Joint."

Stumble's grandmother lived way out beyond the suburbs, and Sticks and the trio had lengthy conversations about why Stumbles visited his grandmother's house so much. The three of the boys accepted the silence, and stared back at one another. If nothing else, just to look at each other enough to think up a quick joke.

Stumbles then hand daps the both of them up as he back pedals across the alley and into the street.

"Sticks?" Stumbles screams out of the window and to Black and Sticks.

"What's up with you, you short shit?" Sticks screams at Stumbles.

Stumbles mom screams, "Watch your mouth boy, before I take you upstairs and clean it out with soap."

"Sorry Mom", Sticks gently screams back as he removes his hat enough to expose his guilty face.

The three mothers of the trio were each boy's mothers in some respect, and the boys in respect for one another, called each other's mother, mom.

"Did shorty call you today?" Stumbles screams back with a smile.

"Oh, that young in' that was at the party last night?" Sticks screams back to Stumbles with a confused look on his face.

"Nah man, this middle finger," as Stumbles replies with a smile, hence dodging the swoops of his mother's round house right hand punch.

Black laughs as Sticks says, "I don't know why I fell for that bogus joke. Stumbles is too short to get some pussy anyway. He's nothing but a virgin." Sticks replies, as the van is towards the end of the block, and headed in the direction of the Interstate, traveling towards Stumbles' peace.

Black smirks in Stick's direction, and then blurts out, "Man, you're always talking about what another dude does." Sticks gives Black that *Who*

Me expression, and without Sticks saying a word, Black says, "Yeah you."

"Who have you done it to Sticks?" Black asks as if Sticks was on the stand, and he was the District Attorney, prosecuting a criminal. The trash cans near the alleyway where they now stood played the jury. The only profession outside of rapping, or being a professional athlete that the boys had always talked about becoming, especially Sticks, was a suit-a man who looks like there are no worries, and drives in the most exquisite cars that couldn't be seen in their neighborhood on a legal engagement.

"I'm getting you ready to become that pimp Joe!"

"Who have you fucked cousin?" Black asks Sticks again.

"Better yet Sticks, what does a pussy look like?" "What does it smell like?" "Come on Sticks, where you at?" The situation gets Black anxious as he hops off of the concrete curb, and is now in Sticks's face smiling, speaking in his best professorial tone. His body language is as serious as the prosecutor staring the witness down for an answer, and affirming the fact that justice is swift and right in front of him.

Sticks stares off as if he is digging into his pile of papers at the hearing stand, and right when he finds the document he was searching for, Black screams out right when Rochelle and Keisha (two High School students) walk past, "Sticks is a Virgin!"

Embarrassed, Sticks says, "Forget you Joe. That's why your underarm hair is as thick as an afro." Sticks get up with dejected body language, and a smirk on his face, and walks up the alleyway.

"Did I hurt your feelings ole' chicken leg?" Black replies with a loud laugh. "I'm just playing cousin! You got to be ready if you're going to be a suit. That's how those dudes are going come at you."

"For Sure!"

Black finishes the statement, and starts to smack the air which plays as the imaginary drum beat that's blaring from the row house they now stood in front of."

Suddenly, the air is broken, as a twenty-one year old woman approaches. Black spoke to her sporadically. She glides out of a nearby house and walked towards the boys. Every now and again, the neighborhood would produce its share of gorgeous women. And regardless of the rumors, prostitution, drug abuse, welfare, and criminal records, the boys respected them all like they respected their mothers. No inappropriate comments to any woman that walked passed. Dependent upon how much they liked them, they would offer to help them with anything that a certain woman might have needed assistance with.

This woman was new to the neighborhood. Her hair was short and it expanded like a full head of broccoli and created a cloud. It was unkempt and as radiant and naturally moistened as a Brazilian woman's hair during Carnival. Her skin peered reflections of Antigua, Cameroon, and Haiti. She topped her love for self by tucking a dandelion in between her ear and the thickness of her fluffy hair. Her white t-shirt irradiated her dark brown nipples as four specks sat atop the rings and mimicked two happy teardrops, bouncing freely atop two perfect spheres. She struck a pose that fingered Black in and kept Sticks captivated. She turned for a moment to look away. Give the boys a peak so they thought. Her waist looked as if she wore a permanent garter. Her bottom dripped slowly towards the base of the hourglass, transforming into an ass that was as wide as the rim on a small yellow school bus' tires. Jeans highlighting how her cheeks clasped under like the smile of a peach, and her feet were not black, nor hard and calloused. The other women's feet were. Walking around the neighborhood bare on the concrete alleyways took its toll. Her feet were as toned as her neck, arms, and wrists. Looking a bit closer, you could see the wet shine of the newly applied toe nail polish. The color on her toes matched the darkness of her nipples perfectly.

Sticks and Black are focused on her for a moment. She's the epiphany of the *Round the Way Girl*.

Black breaks the stare down, and taps Sticks on the shoulder.

"Sticks, that's that Shawty I was telling you about. She is like that! That's sort of how I want my girl to be like."

"I gotta holler at her. Wait right here young." Black made the statement to Sticks as he adjusted his drop socks, fixed the tongue on his timberland boots and tilted the blue Polo cap so that his Afro bush ran under the sides evenly all around.

As Sticks stared at the scene-taking taking place, he heard Black say to the woman, "What's up Shawty. What you need from me?"

Sticks then searches his surroundings atop the curb in the cement alley. Directly behind him were the steel fences, which served as protection to the row houses, which were susceptible to the speeding vehicles that run through the alley from twelve a.m. to twelve p.m. daily. Headlights on his room walls kept him up. Lying on his back in bed, he gained the ability to identify the cars that would travel through the alley nightly.

"At 12:00 a.m." he thought, "a bear growling engine blasts through the alleyway. That's Smitty's truck, a 1972 rickety rusted Chevrolet with a bad exhaust and which is clunky, smelly and loud with intestinal problems."

"At 12:30 a.m., a little click of an engine would come through, with a detail similar to a house on wheels, rocking side to side. It was a stout vehicle, holding too much inside for the body to bear, and it was ready to explode. That would be Clean with the hatch of his Ford Escort open, pumping the radio signals into the house speakers that he installed to replace real subwoofers."

"At 1:00 a.m., or a short time thereafter, a shark would swim through, very quiet and very fast, never waking me. I would actually quell me. My block was safe, and that clarified it. I always dozed off to sleep when I heard it. That was either Real One, or Big T rolling through in their 200ZX with five star rims. You never heard their music, for if they were coming through the alley with no lights on they were creeping for some reason or another."

"Around 2:00 a.m., you can hear the big ship cruise through. Pumping of its gas sounded like the ocean, creating large breaks against the bare project room walls. Gravel underneath its wheels reminded you of a smooth basketball player. He was respected. He might cross you over on the court if you said something out of the way to him off the court. That's a black 1980 Cadillac with a white top, white wall tires and black interior, with diamond stitching. Mr. Galloway owned that car. While eavesdropping on my mother's conversations with Sharonda-our neighbor, Mr. Galloway was doing something with Ms. Belinda across the alley. And he pumps so much gas and speed because he's trying to get home before his wife gets off from work at the hospital. Apparently, he never knew the cars like I did. His wife's Cutlass Sierra would always wait on the corner and speed after him each time around 2:05 a.m."

Other than those cars, I never care about the others, because they weren't from the neighborhood. The music they pumped was different, the volume that they used as they talked, was louder than most, and quite frankly, they had no respect for anyone at 3:00 a.m. Those are the people who probably crashed into the fences. Well, them or Mr. Galloway."

Sticks then turns towards the house separation fences, where some of his friends across the street and in the small courtyard playing baseball with a tennis ball and a broomstick end. Every dude, from the first baseman at the corner clockwise light post that served as first base, to the other two people standing in the street peered serious faces similar to those you would see in a pennant showdown. The faces disclosed the score of the game and inning they were in. Today, they were in the ninth inning with two outs and a loaded set of bases.

Sticks smiled and glanced towards the other end of the alley, where some dudes had tacked a bottomed out milk carton crate to the phone poll, using a plastic football as the basketball. He reflected on the ESPN special on basketball and thought how that scene would make "Pistol" Pete Maravich smile a thousand adoring smiles. The simplicity of the game was at that moment, still the essence of youth, a ball and a basket. No strings attached.

Hot. Walnut and oak trees leaves were a tad brown. The light shade of the trees serenaded the wind. Sticks peered over to a cookout.

Smitty and his family were playing spades and cooking ribs. Earth, Wind, and Fire's *September* was blaring from a three foot and carpeted house speaker. Sticks laughed, as Smitty screamed at a child.

Each time the child went through the door and underneath the cord; his high top hair would hit the cord, and would insight static and disappointment for the folks at the cookout and in the neighborhood.

 "Watch that damn cord, and stop running in and out of the house."

 Steamed crabs with Old Bay seasoning and hints of sprayed Budweiser, resonates as loud as the sirens of the ambulance that breezes down the strip of row houses.

Sticks always dreamed of a big back yard with an expansive green carpet of grass. He sheepishly picks up trash out of other people's grass. This causes him to allude to the spotty grass yards that were taking a pounding from the horseshoe games that were being played on every other back lawn of the row houses.

"Smitty and his family dun created a spot", Sticks thought to himself, as he smiled and waived at Smitty flipping over a rib.

Sticks conceited to his better self and wondered was there anything better than what he was experiencing at that moment. Though he knew there was much more out there, and that it was possible for him to see all there was in the World, he lied to himself, and thought out loud with the statement, "there can't be anything else better than this".

Black smacks the red Ralph Lauren Polo cap off of Sticks's head.

A slap boxing session between the two begins.

With guards up, Sticks asks Black, "Young, what happened to that phat butt?"

As black throws two jabs at Sticks he screams, "Don't worry about that young. You better watch this left and, oops, that right!"

"You always playing you black ass skunk", as Sticks backs up to sit down.

164

"These hands are nice though aint they?" Black throws a straight right jab that land in the middle of Sticks' chest.

Sticks chases him up the alley and leg sweeps Black from behind. Black falls on the only patch of grass left on the playground, which consists of four swings, a Goodyear rubber seat, and a Handful of wood chips. It was an antique sliding board with rickety steps, which ascended at least six feet in the air. The public housing administration must've had a prohibition or budget shortage.

"But who's faster and stronger though nigga?" Asks Sticks, as he triumphantly throws a barrage of punches as Black lays on the ground laughing.

"Stop playing though Young", Black screams as Sticks continues to swing wild jabs.

"For real nigga, before it gets hectic out here." Sticks throws a hand out to help Black up. As soon as Black is on his feet, Pheen Cousin approaches.

Pheen Cousin' was the nickname that they gave to Charles Johnson. He has an uncanny skill of scoring drugs. Back in the seventies, Chuck was the best basketball player around.

Black looks at Sticks and says, "How can you fall so low?"

The story has it that, Pheen Cousin was in his senior year of school. One of the local parochial schools copped him for nothing but a full scholarship. He received offers from a few Atlantic Coast Conference basketball schools. He got his girlfriend pregnant the same year. Making runs to the strip regularly for weed. The puff and give escalated into other things. Two months after finding out that his girlfriend was pregnant, he forfeited the offers and dropped out of school. The rest is history.

Immediately though, Sticks and Black start to laugh.

Almost in complete unison, they scream, "What's up with that eight ball leather jacket player?"

For twenty minutes and a day it seemed, Black and Sticks polished their taunting skills. With peppered barrages directed at Pheen Cousin's out of shape Timberland boots with no laces, cut off jean shorts, lack of a shirt and the audacity to wear an eight ball designed leather jacket on his back in one hundred degree weather, was flat out outrageous. The two boys had found entertainment.

"Main man's mouth smells like he got that black plague."

Black stops his full laugh and giggles at Sticks.

"That cat said that main man breath smell like roach spray." Black tumbles over again in laughter.

Fed up and obviously irritated by the moment, Pheen Cousin interrupts the moment with a shot of reality.

"Yall niggers got big juevos to be fucking with me, you snot nosed ass brats. I remember both of yall niggers when yall was standing in the free lunch line over at the rec. (recreation center)."
"Yall uneducated mother fuckers!"

Pheen Cousin then reaches into is cut off and weathered jean short pocket and pulls out a crisp fifty-dollar bill. A sly grin crosses his face.

Pheen Cousin says to Black and Sticks, "Yall dun got too big for the free lunches huh? Yall niggers got that?"

"We aint got that right now Cousin, but we can get it in a half an hour."

Black whispers the words to Pheen Cousin as the grin turns into a serious stare.

"Yall happy meal eating ass niggers aint gone bust a grape. Why are yall fucking with me right now?"

"Nah nigga, Meet us over by the rec. in twenty minutes." Black replies, and Sticks shakes his head in agreement.

"Are you trying to get some money Sticks?"

Right then and there, Sticks knew exactly what Black was on as he thought about performing the same action. But to dispel the fact, he plays absent minded and doesn't immediately respond to Black. He becomes aloof and distances himself from the reality while concentrating on nothing.

"What you talking about young?" Sticks hesitantly replies.

"Shook One's told me that he be getting main man for mega bucks out they way."
Knowing where this may go, Sticks conjures up a poor excuse.

"Young, I aint trying to rob that nigga, he knows my uncles."

"Young, not rob him stupid. We'll get that nigga something alright."

Black smiled as he rubbed his hands together like a Republican or a corporate attorney salivating.

He found a company worth representing. They have deep pockets.

"How?"

"Easy, follow me to my house."

"Excerpt from a Poem Untitled"

"I am what I am. I am the music that is played, as the poet serenades the mind of a soul untamed. As I wander with the breeze, amongst the high willow trees, to the Heavens my soul is laid. As the mandolin play for a new coming day, I remain a soul unsaved."

Story 8:
A Reprise of Yester-Year:
Vintage Jive

Walking up dark stairwells seems to remind me of a time that I hold dear as we hold these truths to be self-evident. It's dark climbing those stairs, but I was patient enough to wait for what lied ahead. It was my first lesson of delayed gratification. It's the housing projects, or *the projects*, which is synonymous with human hellhole. I will sugar and sprinkle this spice to you folks so that a few of my words won't run the group away. Being there, in the projects, you dig, on any given weekend, was pure bliss. Nothing is different for a brother like me in America. A ghetto this vast land is. The Ghetto! Just as every other community dwellings, *La Nuevo Projectos* - for any of my Latino Brethren- is a microcosm of the big enchilada- America. A ghetto lacks freedom you dig? Notice the fencing that encloses projects. The freedom of thought and expressionism is thwarted by a hustle to make ends meet, and a grind to be ground and possibly chewed and spit out to the heap. This hustle forces many to ignore the vices that clamp the neck of real justice. In the ghetto, justice sees poverty and skin color. Deducing from that that anything therein belongs institutionalized and relegated to the impoverished dwellings, i.e., the projects. One tends to gain the mentality of kill or be killed in the savage jungle of society's sorrows and blues landfills. When expression and freedom is shown, it usually comes out in street ball games. Pimps and hustlers or the wannabe pimps and hustlers are the envied and most hated. Any expression outside the latter is unheard of and never expected. A diamond in the rough is typically smoothed out to the cringing hustle and bustle of the boardrooms or the *real-to-real* rooms; see prisons, or state pens. Around these parts, the ghetto that is, fosters no thought outside the norm. Man, things are exactly the same. This phenomenon is reminiscent of the sub-suburbs-peep my game? Yet, living here fosters "like" relationships and gives folks like me reason. It actually gives living meaning. So *we* stay. Not for any other reason other than to play the script, you follow? "What script? Brother, you might not or better yet, you might want to check your ears. Don't answer for yourself. Put your looking glass on and watch yourself." We play a role. "You be this", and "we are going to be this." "We then have the audacity to pass rolls on from child to child, like Cheadle passes me this super duper grass here.

He takes a deep pull from the white ciga-weed, and the scene changes into a metaphysical pastry.

When you put the cherry on the culinary masterpiece we do it for compensation. And as far as I can see, that compensation is merely an opportunity to state the obvious. "Either you Black, or you white. Now that you have claimed your place on this side, you have the right to profess the obvious to the world." "I mean really, sometimes people get so wrapped in using race and pronouncing it to maintain a status that they forget to shine the basic light which is; what has the person professing their *allegiance* really done positively for their race? God made us all in his image, and imparted us with characteristics that would allow us to adapt to the region that we all lived in. If we were truly hip to the right word, we'd know that we all are the same. Yet, should the shit hit the fan, I know which group I plan on fighting with. And they was the first on this wide, wide Earth, you dig?" "We" are nothing but a throw back to our parliamentary ancestors. The United States middle class are working folks and are all pawns, you dig? We're dancing a sweet, sweet jig for your highness (the top one percent).

Shit, I aint blind, nor am I naïve to believe otherwise. We are compensated with the checks and balances of freedom, pursuits of happiness, in pursuit of a bigger brotherhood that is merely a written script, given by someone else doing the production. Some may profit or *cash in*, but most don't. Those who get that *mean green* can care less about those who don't. And they never will, because caring isn't part of the scripted lines that they received from a generation or two past. Shit, I'm high and even on level ground I would know the real. Plus, I'm one mean motor scooter who has barely made connection with the mother ship.

I have eclipsed the last stair of the mother ship just in time to roll onto the bridge. The sight that I see is such a poetic sight, whatever the word poetic might mean to you. To me, this project house party is sweet poetry. No loud talking. The only thing we all know is that we po', hip' and want some Wild Irish and some wild times. "Classy men and foxy mammas with a twist of some jive time turkeys." Drink on that because I can dig it. Everybody is high on spirits, life or otherwise. I plan to be one of those in that otherwise clique, so I'm wondering what the "flavor of the month" is." Sweet-ass Norma Jean is going to tell it. "Man, Horsefly (aka Willie Lee Davis) just came home from school, he dun ran across that haze, which is as purple as your fat face. Either you hip or just too hip, and by the look of them bell bottomed jeans you got on, you aint hip turkey!!" Norma Jean pimped a sweet stagger away, as she slipped the sister she was with some skin. People are partying for a reason. Dances of jubilee are rampant. Funk echoes that jubilation and the vision of a coming tomorrow. As I sit and watch the happiness on faces, dancers whiz by in their dancing costumes. Fedora's cocked to the side, with jeans that looked as if a tailor had taken a needle to them. Hush puppy shoes and everybody's hairstyle fitted whoever was wearing it. "Willie Dee, we call him", as he slides me some skin. Willie Dee is his name because he is one of them dudes who can shoot a basketball through a concrete net and wet your mamma's finest panties with his cool demeanor, and his hair, which had them natural curls like Billy Dee Williams.

As I look around, I realized that everybody's folks in here go to the same church. Hell, Dean, the cat throwing this party, father is slumped on the china cabinet. I bet he is in that *otherwise* category too.

176

This will be my last thought, for I am spent on talking with myself for the moment. I'm not too much fun, when I'm floating amongst the clouds. I stand to groove to the righteous energy of a many jams as I am swept off of my feet by Constance. Not conscience, but I do realize that everybody's folks are catching hell in their own individual infernos.   The hells were simple, and everyone could spot yours a mile away; the "two job hell, the no food hell, the landlord eviction, and the poor school hell."   We all knew the truth about one another, yet because we were of the same fabric, no one was better than anyone else. We danced for more than the fact that we could dance. We danced for change that we had Faith in and that would come to all of us within this everlasting social struggle.   I can damn sure hear the hell in Curtis Mayfield's throat. Freddy's Dead? Beyond the obvious, you ever wonder who Freddy really was. What he truly and in all best or worst interests stood for? Or do you really care? If you were churned from the same fabric as I, you would use Mayfield's chants of the *Dead Freddy* as your compass for what we're dealing with in this reality.   Though Freddy was part of a movie, that same man in reality is who our kids are looking up to. My momma always told me to pray for the brothers all over the world, for there is a strong chance that they are hearing the blues a lot louder than we are.

As soon as I clicked back to reality, Al Green was telling Connie to lay her head on me. Constance could lie anything of hers on me. She smells sweet, like Cocoa butter and Wild Irish Rose, baby grease, baby powder, a little weed, and a little cigarette smoke. Her breath was like cocoa butter and was as intoxicating as Seagram's Gin to a wino. Before I knew it, I was descending the same stairs and exiting the scene. Connie's old man and mamma went to South Carolina and left her and her brother alone. Corvale was at the party. Corvale is a funny name for a hilarious dude. This cat's like Cosby and Redd Foxx all wrapped up into one. That was his thing, making people laugh, because it forced everybody to forget the gimp leg that he had. You dig? Corvale was on the front line of one of them wars. He didn't last but a month so it seems, as he told us, "Man, either them cats was going to take me out, or them crabs from they women was." "A funny dude", as Corvale was like many of the fellows from around the way. We use our talents to hide the truth, yet won't use them for the good of our community. There are young folks around my way who knows their numbers so well, that they can start their own neighborhood accounting firm. Pimps and hustlers could use their skills to take over companies, and use that money to reinvest back into the communities that they helped to destroy. There are artists who paint the sidewalks with pencils, and could be great art teachers, or great artists, if they only took a moment to expand beyond the institution. This environment allowed the reality to be force-fed to everyone and anchored to their conscious and subconscious. Climbing Connie's stairwell always gave me a righteous feeling for some reason. As high as I was, I had no problem strolling them on any given night. Before I knew it though, Gladys was on that midnight train to Georgia. Minnie was really digging some lucky brother, and Otis was scratched out, as the dock of the bay ruined the flow of the haze. Out of nowhere, I had to do right for Constance and Aretha told me that right was all that I could be. Bliss was blissful. Strolling home, I copped a swig from Wilbo the wino and his quintet. Home, is where the hatred is, you dig? The cats with Wilbo could blow, yet they opted out of the motion picture. The four of them freelance now. Temptation for drugs was the

179

cause of their defection. They probably have seen more temptation that you and I could never imagine. I can't give you the answers to what those people who sift in the murky waters of despair and hopelessness are thinking. Whether you want to or not, you will have to taste those waters and answer those questions under your own guidance. Could you resist the liquor stores on every corner, ten-cent whore on the same corners, racism, unemployment, record stores, ball courts, and nothing more? And on top of that, could you deal with affluent blacks, Asians, and Hispanics calling you a nigger poor?

My evening is over. My old man's crib was where quite a few of up to do black folks had to live. Shit, I'm nowhere up to do, but I'll do, you dig? I plan to flip my script you dig? Let my truths be self- evident. I am the Ikembe pluck to my own jig. Maybe you heard it, and maybe you didn't. Dependent upon the group of folks you recite lines with while acting through this play of life, the message may have just flown over the cuckoo's nest, "Can you dig it, because I can dig it." Sitting at my desk with my crisply pressed suit and attached noose, I wondered, "How in the World did I venture so far from the honest truth?"

While leaving work, I road past a town, only to feel that the place I once knew was rewritten by a different group. A new scene was now the scene, if only they could see the reality and internalize the time that they live in has been instituted to keep them there for generations, ignorant and suppressed. I ascended the stairs at my home, Connie said, "Baby, you alright?" I said, "Yeah, you dig? I was just climbing those stairs again." She smiled.

Story 9:

Eu Nao Estou Enfermo

What a week. It started last Friday. Chloe contacted Stevie to request that I pay her alimony. She feels as though she came away from the marriage with nothing. If it were up to me, she would be paying alimony. I have been working feverishly on getting financial materials out before the tax season at work, and organizing the tax preparation workshop. I haven't had time to speak with any of my friends nor relatives and I received several lengthy e-mails confirming their disapproval. Gloria has been out of the country again, and because she had to stay in London for yet another week, we have lost our seats at the Kennedy Center for the tribute to James Brown. With the week ending on Glo's bad note of news, I unplugged my phone, determined to have this case settled by Friday of next week.

A Week Flies By

It's Friday, 6:30 p.m. and with the Grace of God; I have settled this custody dispute matter. Who would've thought that a custody case could be so intricate?

As I leave the office in midtown and head upper-Northwest for a much needed weekend retreat in my home, I conceited to myself that I hadn't really seen a beautiful spring evening in a while. I started my journey to the Metro Center subway station, at thirteenth and G streets.

Walking along the edges of L'Enfant's town, I realized that I was relaxing, as the contemporary architecture, wooed me in like a clear lens would its photographer. The shutter captured everything in black and white.

It seems that somewhere between a conservative presidency and an undercover republican albeit democratic mayor, the city was frozen in a white state of surprise. The white house and surrounding chess tables, once ordained by street people, were now home to preachers of a different nine to five message. Chest tables were for chest, not cards, nor a bed, nor even a place to eat lunch. It was a place of sane minds, internally politicking to make another move upon a sovereign nation. One side of the street is black, the other side white, both wielding a terrorist passion to check the other into the cheap seats. The thought forced me to think deeper. The time would not allow me to elaborate.

After watching a chest move or two from the new *kids on the block*, I cut down G Street, pass the Old Ebbitt Grill. Weekend revelers started their motorcade towards the back bar. I made a B-line straight to Metro Center.

"What a fucking blow", I thought to myself as the crowded platform waved at me to turn around to a horde of disgusted and impatient faces, gawking at automated signs reading, "Major delays on the Green Line and Red Line trains."

I made a stern turn to the exit, flagged Habib, and rode the chariots of malcontent to my house.

What a week.

I walked up to the doorway, and caught the cherubs atop the door seal smirking down upon me. The mailbox was empty except a few bills and some information that Stevie planned on sending me regarding the new addition to my divorce proceedings.

As I stepped across my threshold, it looked as if I hadn't been home in a week. In essence, I realized that I hadn't been home for a week.

As I dropped my bag, and unlatched my over jacket, I un-tucked my shirt and cuffed my jeans. I then began to clean up my place. All of my dirty socks and old briefs were thrown into the hallway hamper. Dress shirts were tucked away into the bedroom closet. They would meet the dry cleaner another day. Shoes were delicately placed in the bedroom closet on the floor. Brown loafers were with the loafers; the black boots were with the boots, and sneakers with the sneakers.

I made the bed, vacuumed the bedroom floor, and wiped down the bathroom fixtures and mirrors. I also vacuumed the living room floor and straightened chairs. Took all loose papers, and placed them in the inbox atop my desk in the study.

By this time, Platinum Jazz stopped spinning. I plopped onto the couch, with cognac, an ice bucket and speakerphone in tow. Before becoming too complacent, I opened all of the mail and ordered Chinese takeout for delivery. Pepper Steak, egg rolls and fried rice. Check voicemail.

Normally, I hate checking voicemail, because you feel bad for not calling people back. Plus, I always get telemarketers calling and leaving messages.

The First Message:

"Hi, this message is for Theron. I met you at the spot on 14th and U streets. I'm the woman with the big pretty breasts. Remember? I was just calling to tell you that you're a dick for not returning my call last week. And just think, maybe one of these breasts could have been in your…"

I deleted the message.

I thought to myself what I would I say to her; there's a reason why I didn't call you or even call you back. I only spoke to you because I was drunk. Mink, short for Philip Mingus Jessup, is this cat that I went to high school with. He lives in the area and plays crazy games at my expense; plus any woman who approaches you with the introduction line, "hello, my name is P.B.T. - Pretty Brown or Pretty Big Titties"- should not be let out into an adult social setting, let alone a jazz bar. Mink is an old kid and him and P.B.T. would do fine together.

The Second Message:

"You can have the greatest newspaper in the World for less than five cents…."

I definitely deleted the message.

The Third Message:

"Theron," A voice poured through the phone and brought me to attention. The voice was a muted scream and funneling towards a winding highway-somewhere between my place and over yonder. The voice was familiar, and at one time or another and resurrected my spirit immediately. I needed to hear the voice. But who was it I thought?

"Theron, I'm not going to be able to make it back to the States this week…"

I deleted the message as quickly as it rambled on. Glo, called me at work already. Why was she leaving another message? I was really looking forward to the James Brown tribute.

The Fourth Message:

"Theron, I knew that you were going to delete my previous message."

I smiled.

"This is Glo, and initially I thought that I would have to stay for another week. As it turns out, I will get back in town tonight (Friday) just in time for our normal tapping sessions. By the way, I picked you up something from Pink. I will be flying out in an hour. I can't wait to see you.... bye, bye."

As I deleted the message, my energy immediately perked up, and I felt compelled to check the remainder of my messages before catching a couple of TV shows.

The Fifth Message:

"Theron (pause), this is Lindsay. I have no idea why you've been ignoring me. I'm guessing you've been busy at the office. Next time Negro, call me back. Well (pause), I have something to tell you. Because I have tried your house six times, this being the first in which I've left a message, I hate leaving you this unsettling statement on the phone. I will be flying overseas for a short time, as my new friend (giggles) Mitch has invited me to spend some time with him at his villa in Tuscany. Mitch and I have been seeing each other for the last two months. Well not seeing, but we have been out enjoying life together. And though I don't have to tell you about this, I felt compelled to do so, because I love you and want you to know that regardless of what may happen in the next six months, I will always love you. Theron.... (Sobs) Goodbye."

I dropped the phone, in utter disbelief. I thought that I had found my soul mate. I thought that we were giving each other space to organize our lives, with the anticipation of possibly one day rekindling our relationship. Lindsay is leaving me. She's moving on.

I sat there on the couch in silence for fifteen minutes. Silence was broken by the busy tone blaring from the speakerphone, which in reality was screaming at me and mocking me, while urging me to hang up the damn phone.

Who in the world is Mitch? She has never said anything to me about a Mitch, and for the last two months she was telling me that she was busy working. I had hundred's of questions, i.e., where's her daughter, how's her housing situation coming, how's her divorce coming, how does she really feel about this dude?

I frantically reached for the headset to the phone, and dialed her numbers as quickly as death will dial my own one-day. The voice mail picked up, and with welling eyes, I paused after the beep. No words, and pressed the goodbye button.

After the Fifth message, there were five more. It's at these times when you realize that you know more people than you thought.

The Tenth Message:

In a forthright and smoky tone, "ah there, this is Cy (Cyrus Q. Coles). I know we haven't had a conversation for a while dog, but I have a crucial story to share with you about my trip to Brazil. Hit me man, when you get this message. Peace."

"Weird", I unconsciously muttered out loud. I hadn't had a deep conversation with Cy since we were both in graduate school. One must lose dependency in order to move forward. You can only bounce ideas off of the same group of people for so long. You have to take those ideas and put them to action. In many ways, Cy helped to mold my persona, whether I wanted to accept that or not. In many ways, Cy was one of my good friends. Because of the tone of his voice, I probably should call him back. But not before I listen to the next few messages.

The Eleventh Message:

"Theron, what's up my man? Still working those long hours huh? This is Cy again. I just left this party. The drinks flowed freely. The music quelled my soul. The women were extraordinarily stuck up. I suppose you have to wear gaudy jewelry to holler. Anyway, hit me man, so I can get your updated information. I have pictures from Brazil that I want to e-mail you. Plus the story I have is unreal. Hit me. Peace."

Cy is still out doing his thing. I could never fault him for getting out and being him. Even in college. My friends relished Bachelorhood. I always wanted a family, always wanted to be a family man and always wanted to be a father. I think that the more I wanted to be a family man, the more the reality of doing so became unattainable.

The Twelfth Message:

"Theron, hello, oh damn, that's your answering machine again. Hit me man…this is Cy. Peace."

"Wow!" I sighed out loud, as I realized something was up with Cy.

I ran to the study to retrieve Cyrus' phone number, and returned his call.

The phone ranged four times and suddenly the voice mail chimed in. Coltrane's *Afro Blue* set the tone of his voicemail."

"This is Cy Coles, I'm not able to get to the phone, please feel free to leave me a message. Peace."

"Cy, this is Theron. Nice music. I've been holed up in the office for the last week. Hit me and let me know what the deal is with you. I'm pumped to hear about the trip to Brazil."

I then hung up the phone.

I pushed the goodbye button on the headset, and hopped up to go to the bathroom. As soon as I hit the bathroom door, the phone ranged. I picked up the headset from the wall, as I relieved myself.

"This is Theron."

"What's up Bro?" were the words that I heard from the other end.

"Hey." I hesitantly replied, as I had no idea who it was.

"Man, how's life in Washington?"

Again, I hesitantly said, "its peace." Right when I said the word peace, I missed the toilet, and screamed, "Damn!"

"What's wrong with you?" was the question that came forth from the other end.

"I missed the fucking toilet."

We both start laughing hysterically

"What's up my man Cy?"

"Man, just living and enjoying the sun. When you called before, I was in the bathroom doing that in which you can't miss the floor."

We both start laughing hysterically again.

"I got to get out of here in about a half an hour to catch Brazzaville, live."

"Whoa, Brazzaville is in the country?"

"Yeah Bro, They have a New York show in about a month. I'll forward you that information over e-mail. Oh, by the way, you didn't mind me getting your e-mail from the Alumni directory, did you?"

"No, not at all Cy, in fact, I had no idea that the directory had my e-mail information. Nevertheless, the picture was off the hook. From what I was looking at, the dames down in Brazil were rear heavy."

"Yeah, Man. The heaviest rears and fronts you can imagine. But none of those pictures can account for the time I had there."

"It was that crucial?"

"Theron let me tell you."

"First, two dudes from work, Chip and Reed, decided out of nowhere that because the workload was so low, that we would take a trip."

"Holmon & Dunn must be paying you well these days."

"That's besides the point dog! So out of the blue, while at a bar, Reed's girlfriend Carla comes into the bar and starts to curse him out."

"For what?"

"We never knew why, but they ended up breaking up. They had crazy trust issues, she was controlling. Reed was too passive. Reed probably isn't ready for marriage anyway. I can see him and Carla reconnecting. So of course, Reed was blown. He wanted to propose to Carla in Sao Paulo, Brazil of all places. He brought two tickets to do so during a sunset, in Sao Paolo."

"This all happened in February?"

"Yeah, so Reed is blown and everything, and of course Chip and me was hyping him to forget about her and prepare ourselves to travel. An hour or so passed in the bar, and we're all obliterated. The three places that we all had chosen were Amsterdam, Prague, and Jamaica. Of course, I chose Amsterdam, Chip chose Prague, Reed Chose Jamaica. After another hour, we couldn't come to a conclusion, because of money issues, timing restrictions, and availability. So out of nowhere, Reed says, "Fuck it, how about the three of us split the price of one ticket, and someone can fly for free using Carla's ticket? So Chip and I are like, "lets plan for next month, we'll have our spring bonuses by then, and we can all roll." Now Reed is a junior partner at he firm, and in his drunken stupor, he's like, "fuck spring bonuses fuck next month. Let's roll Friday."

"Theron?"

"Wow!"

"Theron, it was Wednesday."

"Next thing I know, I'm drunk, high off the nicest green I've had in a while, and flying out of

Houston International. I dozed off to Reed and Chip finishing their last project for work."

"I awake to laughing, as Chip and Reed are giving me shit for not knowing enough Portuguese to understand that we are ten miles from Rio's International Airport, and everyone's seat is upright. I'm still wrapped up in my blanket with a pillow beneath my head."

"As I rush to get prepared for descent, Reed says, "Hey dick, lift your shade and check out Christ the Redeemer. Theron, that was the first time I though that maybe, just maybe, I was about to enter Heaven.'

"Upon getting off of the plane, Reed had purchased an escort service for the week to drive us around. We had reservations at two hotels near the Ipanema and Copacabana beaches. Dependent upon which one was the nicest, that's where we would stay."

"Brazil is absolutely an ill country. Despite the fact that you definitely see the impoverished immediately, running some type of game or another, you also see the many different colors of the Brazilians. Dark skinned, brown skinned, mulatto, whites, Man, Brazil is ill."

"Cy, that sounds crucial. How long you did stay there, a week?"

"Yeah, but that really isn't all that I have to tell you."

"Oh, what else went down?"

"So after four or five hours of gawking at the most luscious and fruitful asses on earth-I mean the women had the bottoms of perfect peaches- we decided that we would stay near Copacabana, and move to the hotel near Ipanema by mid week. Ducasse Rio Hotel is where we checked in. The people in Brazil are mad friendly, as one hotel worker, Pasquel, offered to show us around for an evening, for fifty American dollars of green, ten American dollars of ecstasy, and two newspapers later. O Globo and the Journal do Brasil with real. Real is Brazil's currency. So like crazy assess we did."

"As we got settled into our room, the three of us took a piece of each newspaper, each of us rolled a phat one, and we all checked the current events, for the happening spots, just in case Pasquel pulled a game on us. No one except Reed knew Portuguese, so we just looked at the places where we saw Brazilian women, which normally was a signal for erotic massages or escort services."

"The green was fire, and after smoking a fat one, I passed out. Once again I awoke to Reed and Chip out on the deck screaming at a few big bottom hotel maids. As I looked out the window, and onto the beach, my eyes only saw cheeks in thongs. The sight was sick my man, sickness."

"Theron, are you still there?"

"Yeah man, go ahead."

"I'll shorten the story. So for the rest of the night, we just ran around taking pictures on the beach and getting nice on green and mostly domestic Brazilian rum. So it was probably one thirty to two o'clock in the morning, and after all if the choice sights walking around, you can only want to entertain a few. So rather than pulling a few, we headed to Lido, which is on the border of Copacabana."

"What's Lido?"

"Man, Lido is Copacabana's red light district. For some crazy reason, Reed convinced Chip and I to drop the Ecstasy that we copped. We did, and the heightened urge to score, became a necessity. Mentally nice, and observing all of the prostitutes walking around, Reed is asking around for a nice Termas, which really means an exotic spa or a code word to relax. So out of nowhere, someone taps me on the back, and I'm, so nice that I didn't have a clue if it was a prostitute or what, but I turn around, and with a tanned smile on his face, Pasquel screams, "what the deal my main man?"

"So we all have our moment of excitement as Pasquel has obviously delved into his own stash, and then his face turns devious."

"So you boys want to have some fun huh? In unison, we say, "yeah!"

"Pasquel, then says, "Follow me!"

"We walk along the worse stretch in Lido. It was too seedy to really stop, so in a straight line it seemed, we sped the pace to the spot."

"After Reed and Pasquel approached a red door with two men standing outside of in dark suits, they happily waved us to come in. Reed slid the men something in their hands, and it seemed that we jumped from the frying pan and right into the fire."

"Four women approached us with white slippers and white robes. We joined a host of other men dressed in robes and slippers, those rich and poor. Distinguishable only by the language they spoke or the foreign money that they tipped the almost naked waitresses in the room."

"I was still smacked off of the E, and I could tell that Chip, Reed and Pasquel were still high as well. The place was a lounge type of place with vintage wooden tables with glass tops, and red walls. There were large pool tables, and bar stools with some sort of fur on the seat. The women serving drinks were better looking than a lot of the women that you see on T.V. and their bodies rivaled any everyday phat black woman that you might find walking the streets of New York or D.C."

"So, to induce the high that we already are on, Pasquel, purchase a round of Red Bull and Vodka, and drops a new dose of E in each. The music which was a low key hum, now changed to an up tempo Bossa Nova/Calypso tune, and before I knew it, hordes of women with nothing but see through gowns and smiles to die for came peeling down the stairs. Everyman in the room grabbed someone, and as quickly as the room was full of men, gorgeous and naked women overran it. Pasquel and Chip were clapping hands feverishly as two twins approached them. They waved at Reed and I and were off upstairs. A toned dark skinned woman, with nice calf muscles, an all right ass, huge breasts and long flowing hair approached Reed. If here skin were three shades lighter, her ass a little smaller and her tits a little bigger, she would look like Carla. But I couldn't hate on Reed, as he happily dapped me up and headed upstairs."

"What about you?"

"So I'm standing there, and for some reason, all of the ghetto Brazilian women approached me, and asked me questions in broken English about Tupac, Biggie and Jay-Z. One even proposed marriage. All of them were phat, but I have slept with some phat borderline ghetto women back in the States. So I coasted around the spot, bumming a cigarette and copping feels from the various ladies who approached me."

"Finally exhausted from looking for that right one to spend my money on, I sat down and enjoyed the rest of my high. Listening to Antonio Carlos Jobim sing over a semi Afro-Cuban tempo put me in that zone. And as soon as I got there, I found her."

"Cy, what she look like, how'd she look?"

"Theron, she was like five foot five, a white Brazilian, with hair down to the small of her back. Her teeth gleamed as clean as ivory, C cup breasts, and her butt was the closest thing to a human peach that I had ever seen. She comes up to me takes my cigarette and throws it on the ground. She puts both my hands on her butt cheeks and in an educated, yet broken tone, she says, "I want you".

"How could I deny this I thought? So we climb the stairs, and go into this room. The room was standard, yet from the window, you could see the beach. She went to a radio and put on Bebel Gilberto, and started to dance. She then bent over, and in front of the window, and started fanning it from West to East. I dropped my robe, and put on a condom, but before I could get in on, she falls on the bed and is doggy directly in front of me. Yo, it was spread and red like a pomegranate fruit, oozing nectar. Sweet seeds ready to be popped and savored. So, I put the condom on, and started to do my thing. For an hour we did our thing."

"Towards the end of the session, I pulled out because I was about to bust off for the eighth time it seemed, when I felt a drip into my hand."

"Cy, go ahead man, don't say that."

"Yeah man, the condom broke. The music stopped right there and then. Silence came over me, and I froze. She knew it, and got up in a fever to wipe herself, and she started to cry."

"Cy, I mean, what did she say to you?"

"She said, Eu Nao Estou Enfermo! Eu Nao Estou Enfermo!"

"Theron, I got to roll man, I can't be late for Brazzaville. I'll hit you in a week or so."

"Damn", I thought, as I said, "cool man. Cool." And we both hung up the phone.

There were two knocks at my door. I suspect it's either Gloria or the Chinese dude.

Reality Check:
The Final Blessing

I can never fully interpret this strange dream called life. Every time that I feel as though I have a firm grip on this paradigm, reality seeps through my hands like sand through a flour sifter, slowly and accurately. Reality trickles and I am back at square one. The beautiful epiphany that comes from that loss is what I like to call a "new birth". That new birth is the realization that though the sand you once owned trickles from the palm of your hands and into oblivion, so it seems, your imprint is left upon the beaches of reality for someone else to sift through and find something of use. That square one is the new birth of understanding. During my time in Washington, D.C., I learned that through the journey of finding yourself, you must experience emotion, various feelings, and various perspectives, which ultimately comes from the mistakes and triumphs that you have in interacting with several people. For what it is worth, my experience seems to float through anyone that I come in contact with, and ultimately myself.

In offering the sand that I had collected and clutched snugly in my satchel, I expected to receive something in return for those people that I walked with through the journey called self-discovery. Sometimes, for random people, self-discovery becomes an oxy moron, as people and society on a whole helps to mold ones scope of self-discovery. That philosophy may very well appeal to everyone. The only problem that lies within the philosophy of accepting others *leftovers* are that because the offering did not come in the form that I imagined it would, I closed my ears and became deaf to the rhythm played on my behalf. Meanwhile, each of those teachers gave me insight into my own psyche in their own way, and without knowing one another.

I have found that losing dependency and structure through friends, family, co-workers, or what have you, is the best therapy to learning how to float on your own. Throw a novice swimmer into a pool of metaphysical sharks and bet your life savings that the novice swimmer will no longer be considered a beginner after the experience. That is how I perceive Life to be. Put on blindfolds, think clearly, and run like hell, meanwhile, leaving Faith to God and his momentary reason. The irony in this whole ordeal is that as my friends and associates showed me to me, and I saw those needed adjustments, my World began to gel together.

When I feel a shift in my own personal being, I will once again be at square one, waiting for yet another new birth. And if I was seventy years old and reading this, I would call this growth, even though it seems that I am far beyond what I was mentally, years ago. In the meantime, and before its time to once again look deep into myself, I want to thank those worth the thanking and thank those who may not be worth the thanking. Without the entire gamut of outside circumstances and individuals, those associated with triumph and defeat, there will never be a complete me, or for those who can relate in any way, a complete you.

Story 10:

Brutal Sanctuary

He sat there along the sandy edges of the Potomac shoreline, which was five miles north of the Mount Vernon plantation. Ten paces from Privet's Point, a bird sanctuary. The moist spring air extenuated his heavy rasp. Exhaled carbon dioxide diced into the evening dusk, floating overcast. Smoke from a mint cigar. His unkempt and un-tucked shirt was as wrinkled as the flock of exotic geese. The geese completed the tapestry that spanned above the edges of the sun-setting horizon. He raised his head, and from his glossy and fiery eyes he stared across the Potomac with welling waters of pain wielding him blind to his surroundings. His eyes focused downwards to the center of his palms, while concentrating on the swooping *M's* stamped along the sky, those that he raised to the Heavens. Had he taken a moment to research his metaphysical lifeline, he might have seen this moment coming.

Every sound he heard was equated to distant reflections and each sound concocting an explanation for his unwanted anguish. The wayward ambulance siren, far from its hellish jurisdiction, resonated in his mind. As loud as the harpist that he sat and admired during a lunch hour in Washington Square. Oblivious to the fact the real love knows no barrier, and upon opening his eyes, she sat there beside him. Her mulatto-Creole legs fell from her conservatively fitted red skirt. Her hands gently raised a turkey, provolone, romaine, and tomato on croissant, to her red and symmetrically perfect and full lips. The corners of her mouth clasped like an inter-changeable gadget of some sort. Her face poured back into the crashing spirals of wormy curls as she coyly asked him for a napkin. His embroidered handkerchief was raised from his heart's pocket, and given to her, as her mulatto face blushed with happiness.

As she passed him his handkerchief, he gently folded it and placed it snugly in his hip suit pocket.

The tide began to crash into the Potomac shoreline as a few more tears rolled down his face. The crashing of the tide was similar to the moment his heart fell to his stomach when she told him that she was seeing another man, and that the two of them, her and he, would only be friends. He accepted the fact, because though he took her to a coffee shop (his favorite), a few baseball fields (his favorites), and the greatest of all, his weed spot (distributor of his peace), she had unknowingly walked down a few corridors of his heart and soul. Few people had ever walked that far, nevertheless, he dug her, if for nothing more than her willingness to experience his personal grace. Out in the distance, his blurred vision spotted speckled perch, and jealous cat fish leaping atop the redden horizon. The slapping backs of animals and water forced him to reflect on the elation of his friendship with her becoming more than a friendship-her and Real, as in Reality C. Ross-broke it off, and she was willing to start something anew with him.

As he stared down at his watch, the dial read six twenty seven, as he further conceited to himself that time flew past, regardless of the emotion involved in the moment. That thought placed him retrospectively into another country with the woman he came to appreciate. He loved this woman, and marveled at her personal grace as he watched her posing for black and white shots against the Paris backdrop. He laughed as she heckled the Saturday street merchants, which was two blocks southeast of La Gar Saint Lazare.

He couldn't believe that six hours from that moment would bring another day. And not just another day, blessed by the love of God, but another day of longing. That emptiness, devoid of the love he gave, was the same space that he yearned to fill each time he brought her trinkets. Pick nicks in the park, dinner at his cabin, and these gestures never got him a moment more each time he requested her love. She opened up his doors of security as they toasted with her friends in Las Vegas, and sailed for a week along the coast of Brazil. He could never fit in with any of them. Not because of money or even because of education, but because of the soul in his walk, his talk, and the movements in his gestures. They could not relate to him or him to them. Stevie Wonder was more than an artist to him. During certain points in his life, Stevie was his father, thus showing him the world through a muted visual matrix. He was his friend, and the one who gave him his first glimpse of love and heartbreak. The World is really a jungle. A prophet, Stevie saw the World better than he did as a man having sight. Marvin Gaye was more than a troubled entertainer to him. Marvin was a guide on how to be conscious in the Jungle, while loving the people that they may come across during their time on Earth. "Maybe", he sarcastically said out loud, shortly before he took a swig of the dark nectar, extracted from the barrels of aged oak. "Maybe things could have been better." He thought back to many indiscretions he had gone through and turned a deaf ear to, just to appease her.

He felt sharp pains in his chest, as the anxiety built. The pains were exactly like those he felt when he found her curled in bed, lifeless so it seemed. Only when he frantically shook her arm did he realize that she was only sleeping. Sleeping from her previous indiscretion, for the drug she took for momentary pleasure, she now took for pain, strength and happiness, which was devastated by the unwanted growth. Deep down parts of her removed. Tumultuous waters no longer raged therein. What bound them together she threw away and abandoned her. He never abandoned her, despite that reality.

As he staggered up the slope, along the Potomac shoreline, he got into his car and sped down the parkway headed opposite of Mount Vernon. Swerving in and out of control, the car veered sporadically in and out of opposite flowing traffic. He unconsciously flirted with death. As he realized his near demise, he pulled over for a moments rest, before awakening to two familiar, yet blurred faces. They shouted obscenities to him. He morphed back into the Greek inspired restaurant that he recommended to her. With engagement ring in tow, it was her who strolled in. Radiant as the day the harp gently lured her into his life, accompanied with the man whom she still confided in daily. He whom she still thought had a deeper purpose in her life. And with the loud blare of a wayward fugal horn, she told him that they were too different to be a couple. The two of them, he and her will forever be friends. She then turned and sat down with Real for dinner.

As he stepped out of the car with one hand behind his back and the other tipping the dark oak, his uncle and older brother stood there to snatch the drink and to catch him by the arm pits if need be. Instead, he stepped out of the steaming car. Walking the straight line, together, they guided him into the house where they laid his dejected body onto the couch. He opened his blurry eyes, dumbfounded and disorientated, and caught the image of his twelve year-old self atop the fireplace. He dozed off to sleep.

Along the sandy edges of the Potomac shoreline, four miles north of the Mount Vernon plantation, and ten paces from Privet's Point- a bird sanctuary, he awakens muddy and wet from the now fallen April rain.

"I must have fallen asleep sometime ago."

It was midnight, barely another day, and whether the day was real or imagined; he tossed a small black bow, with a special ribbon attached, into the Potomac River. He cracked open another bottle of cognac for the ride home. He strolled up the hill, without worry, care, nor aspirations on his mind.

Story 11:

The Birth of Ambition

She, the older woman-not in the physical, but in the mental, walked like Heaven. The embodiment of all her creator had to offer. Sometimes, she would make me question whether God was really a woman. The bitch was stunning to the eye. We walk by Faith and not by sight. She is captivating in her witty ways, coupled with her feline demeanor, and she was always enticing her foes to speak and encouraging her lovers to shy away. Who is she, but a woman confused? Or is she cunning enough to persuade others to purge her anxieties? Her voodoo sends others to handle her dirty work, thus recouping emotional and mental tariffs for not recognizing her mojo from day one. I recognized and wanted her. I was too young, so she said.

To an old boy, she could become the sun or a wayward light that would offer me a last piece of guidance. Unlike any man she conquered and rendered subservient to her play, I caught her vibe in her best and worst moods. I jotted down her thoughts from every conversation that we had, never on paper, only upon the written ledger of my mind. I promised myself that I would figure her out, while learning what the prefect man meant to her, while also knowing that foot massages were a doorway to her. She kicked me, spat on me and ran me ragged. The game that she started was ten innings. She was throwing a shutout for the first two. She dropped her guards, and introduced me to friends. I being the student dialed in to her every intricate detail. Down to the D cup and twenty-three inch waistline. I searched and studied. No man thought as deep as I was willing to. No man even dared to test her. From her conversations, you would've thought, she left dictators, presidents and CEO's weak. And upon figuring out her game, a game she played, denying that it was even a game, I, the old boy, was ready to counterattack. There was a reason that she led men to believe they were inadequate. They weren't. They actually showed that weakness to her, never confronting those inadequacies in front of her. Allowing her to play her hand, I, the old boy, no older than a legal drinker, boasted about my physical prowess. It was true that what hung below, could work the longest of the longest, graveyard shifts. I knew that what her mind wanted to do, her body could not. I knew that each man before stopped when she stopped and rested when she did. Gave in when she thought it was pertinent to give in. Smitten with the possibility of falling for an old boy, she realized that all that I professed to her was true.

Most men, careful to set her off, allowed her to smack them in the face, when they were wrong, rendering to her the upper hand. And if she even raised her hand to me I planned to retaliate, mentally. I was a reminder of a yesteryear; when one of her young intimate friends would grab her in one of her tantrum spells, fuck her brains out. Shower her off. Send her home happy and apologetic like the naughty girl she was. Emotionally, as a chocked throat would hit a sentimental note when explaining to her my plight, she likened my episode to violins serenading the background. In reality, Biggies Smalls was blasting through my mind and I knew I had her despite what her face told me. I would snatch the loot. Physically, age was the one thing that she feared yet loved so dearly. My youth left her curious and fearful of what pleasure and pain I could inflict upon her.

I, the old boy, no older than a legal drinker, knew that I had her. Calls were frequent; dates were being planned for her and I. Her switch was no longer of a wise goddess but that of a wise femme fatale. All men recognized. Her walk told the truth of a story so dark and deep, that for years the façade that she kept up was now crumbling. The reality and the character of her many convictions shined through. She craved for me- my good and young energy. I, the old boy, became hip to the fact that I was now winning the game. Seal my efforts. Sharing a few nothings to her closest friend on what I imagined she would like someone to say about her. Fully knowing that what I would say would return to her no slower than the blink of an eye. What she would hear would be more than men her age would ever say to her. Physically, mentally, spiritually and emotionally, I had her. She knew it, and all of those around her knew that the light in her eyes reflected a young glow-a twice-reworked light. And in giving the older model a new drive, they still couldn't touch the luster and amenities of the newer model, especially when a girl wanted to go for a long ride. Out along the countryside, where the sun's hot and the days long. There's nothing to do but lie in the grass and realize what real pleasure is.

I laid her in her bed. She couldn't believe that what I told her I would do with her some months ago was done. She is happier than she had been in some time. I kindly looked over at her soft golden side, and extended my arm over her warm and sweating body.

"My dear, not unlike anything else in my life, what has happened between you and I is due to my burning desire."

On the same page, she backed herself up, and turned towards me over her golden shoulder.

"Isn't that what you men call ambition?" I nodded, thus in concurrence with her sentiment. From that day, I knew and understand ambition, as she taught it to me.

Story 12:

Passover

He lies on the silver bed surrounded by
pumps and pressure gauges. Stale air mixed with
the effervescence of death. His arm, bludgeoned
by pricks from pine needles he once thought,
which were birthed by the leftover scrap from
steely knives that pierced his outer skin. They
allowed his body to rest easy, and for him to nod
and free fall to his inner core. There, deep down
beyond the cavernous pits of gas and flesh, he
could escape the pain of the World. Sort of like
death, except in not knowing death, he could only
attribute that inner space as a doorway into the
internal light, which left him paralyzed. Though
he had condemned those users he had seen, he
now knew what intravenous drug users felt when
they took their first rush of adrenaline. Anything
thereafter could never kill the urge of that first hit
of escape.

It had been four weeks, he thought, since he had
left the mortal wing of the hospital. Those rooms
had windows for nostrils, which inhaled and
exhaled gentle breezes, and blew back cut grass
blades. Those nostrils doubled as eyes.
Sometimes color blind, he could still distinguish
between the squirrel and rabbit. They kindly
encouraged him to get better. The sunshine was

companion enough. It was there where he clung to the hope that a scalpel, some morphine or chemo, would quell the venomous cancer. Instead, the vipers grew and slowly and precisely unleashed their venom from his colon, to his lung, gently squeezing the passion of life from his soul. That is where there was hope- family and friends. They came often to talk of the World and its politics. He was a prisoner, devoid of the realities that surrounded him-as Faith would have it, he would not be granted parole, probation, or maybe even a pardon. He was unconscious of the times that moved feverishly and steadily. The ides of father times antique pocket watch-relegated him to solitary confinement. He was unable to physically go to the yard to exercise. Raped by the mentality of the system and of due time, he could only lie there, read, and breath oxygen. Like it or not, he was preparing for his own Passover.

It was there. He could remember the sermons he would give to the people. He had been a preacher, and from the pulpit he would scream and shout onto the disciples. Warning of grave futures, while instilling hopes of self-salvation. In between each breath, he would write in the column of his notes, questions of whether fear was a better tool than hope. He would stand before the same group of people, and guide an ascended soul to Heaven. Maybe he'd reprimand a descended soul to hell, though he never judged.

"Before a single stone is cast, speak if there is a man here who has never sinned."

A passage he lived by, so careful to speculate, he knew better. For each funeral that he presided over, the very first to his last one some two months ago, he realized that he was the final equalizer between a soul's ascension to Heaven and departure to Hell. As far as he knew, that soul had already made her wager some years before, either to the God of Christ, or the God of Sodom. That person had rolled the dice for whatever their heart desired here on Earth. Yet, he always tried to get them through to everlasting glory. He always prayed equally when presiding at a funeral, whether for the old to the young. Fool to the wise man and saint to the sinner. And like the people who stopped visiting when his soul and body had reached their collective critical capacities, he would leave the church and walk along the Potomac to ease the pressures of the World.

He was sixty pounds lesser than his one hundred and sixty pound body had been for twenty some odd years. His name was Pastor C.T. Wilton II. He was a third generation pastor from Lanham. Maryland and graduated at the top of his class from Howard University. He received his call to preaching while lying face first in the bathroom in a jazz nightclub in Kansas City, Missouri. Somehow, he found that either he would follow the rest of the jazz band and their destructive ways, or follow God. He married at the age of twenty-six, to his wife of forty three years, Sister Alma C. Wilton. He met that very night, coming from the bathroom, realizing that he had but one hundred dollars, his horn, his clothes and a smidgen of pride. They bore seven kids, two doctors, Lloyd R. Wilton, M.D. and Sandra Wilton-Washington M.D, two lawyers, Paul L. Wilton, Esquire, and Luna (Lue) Wilton-Haltom Esquire, one jazz musician, Romelo M. Wilton, one school teacher, Mary D. Wilton, and his splitting image, Wilton III, whom he hadn't seen nor spoken to in five years. He deemed himself a renaissance man and international playboy.

He was awakened by the sound of shoes shuffling across the floor in his room. The sound reminded him of a funeral, and thereto, he knew that his time was near.

He introspectively prayed, "Dear Lord, of all that you have blessed me with while on this long and everlasting journey, I ask for but one thing. For I know that once I profess it in your name, you will grant me this blessing. Please give me the strength to see my family one last time, and to prepare myself for my journey home- Amen."

With the little strength that he had, he waved his wife to adjust his pillow, and he gingerly increased the oxygen which was pure life wheezing through his nozzle.

The attorneys approached him, both saddened and ashamed of themselves. And like the many days that he coached them through their trials and tribulations, he took a swig of oxygen, released his mask, and asks with a smile, "How's lady Justice?"

Half laughing, half thinking about how they would cope without their center of sanity, they both sat there and stared in his tired eyes. Without a word, he glanced back and saw Paul and Luna standing over him at the ages of seven and nine. The look they peered was the same then as it was at that particular moment.

The look asked the man on his bed the question, "When will you get well so that we can play?"

And unlike then, the father glanced back, and said, "My children, there is nothing you nor I can do. And not unlike many other times, this will probably be the last time you will talk to me. As I told you Paul your first year of law school, and you Luna, during your Masters classes, walk by Faith and not by sight. Though I am weak in the flesh, I am strong in the spirit. And though you are weak in the spirit find comfort in he who will receive me. Paul, I see that you are about to cry."

Silence ensued, and never, since Wilton III pushed Paul down at the playground, did he show weakness. Neither in court, nor when he was ridiculed being the only black kid on the crew team. He never wavered when he was ostracized while in law school, and before he was partner at the firm. Now he cries, as if he had never cried all of his life. Paul kissed his father and exited the room.

Winton II takes another shot of oxygen and pastes his practiced smile, and gently grabbed the hair of his beloved Luna. As her lips quivered, and gently opened, words could not pour forth.

"Daddy's little girl." He grimaces, and the family rushes to the bed. He waves everyone away as if he was still the earthly commander and chief of his own family. The commander and chief of his own soul, and his own body. He pushes the blinking button that he clutched for dependence, and that released a little elixir that quelled the pain.

"Now where were we baby doll? I read your e-mail you sent me. You give me strength! I love you, and rather or not I'm here with you now and gone later, or here for yet another day, you must clutch and claim your Faith in him. Not me, for I am of flesh. You wonder why you haven't won a case in several tries, and why you haven't found a man that is worth you staying with forever. It's because you must trust in him, and only him. No man, no money, no career, nothing of this World can possibly give you the security and Wealth that he can deliver. Now give me a kiss, and go comfort Paul. You two have always been peas in the pod!" She kisses her father, and like clockwork, Paul grabbed his sister and wiped her eyes, and Winton II grew warmer, gained confidence, and loved his persona more. He realized that though he was prepared to leave his body, he would always remain on Earth through his kids, and their kids.

Lloyd and Sandra then glided to the bed. Winton II likened them to the final two doctors that he would see while eclipsing his check out time here on Earth. They both carried the same looks as his doctors, and through life never really showed compassion toward anyone but ailing people. They were distant children and bookworm adolescents, who would become devout Christians. Always taking the Lord with them, they were dedicated humanitarians and wonderful human beings. Winton II smiled and said to both, "Docs, how much time do I have left?" They looked at him, both half-heartedly showing laughter, repeated in unison what they had told him at the ages of twelve and thirteen when their dad asked then, "Dad, we human's don't have any time. For anytime might be that time." They smiled and both in unison, clutched their dad's hands, and performed all of the technical comfort exercises that even a seasoned nurse could never perform.

"Now go and comfort your brother and sister, for they need the two of you more than for Sunday dinners and holidays. They were never as strong as the two of you. But let me let you two in on a secret; Paul cried tonight"

They smirked and nodded and hand in hand, they strolled out to clutch the naps of their brother and sister who looked through the rectangular windows.

Winton II dozed off to Alma's humming, as she rubbed his hand and read Psalms into the room. A few hours had passed and Alma now slept on the empty bed across from her husband. The children had all fallen asleep in the lobby, as the grandchildren curled underneath arms, chairs and a sink. All of the grandchildren, wondering when grandpa would get up and give them a dollar or a pat on the head for speaking properly.

As Winton sat up, his heart began to race, as a shadow arose in the corner. The shadow had a black hat, a Fedora, and a black suit. A silver something. Piercing micro crystals-a tune that he once played to his son from his horn blared back in his direction, which was fiery and forceful, melancholic, sad, albeit hopeful. The tune was toned down, and Winton II closed his eyes, and reminisced on his days as a jazz musician. His son, Romelo, played for his father for twenty minutes, as the music mixed with his tears, and cried from his weary soul. Somehow his cold demeanor brightened the dark room. At the end of the song, Winton II tried to speak, but no longer could. And even with three more hits of morphine, he could not say a word. Romelo, walked over and said, "Dad, don't strain. I can see it in your eyes. I can see your joy, I can see your Grace, and I can see your fear. And guess who taught me how to read eyes? You pop, when I was fifteen, and was about to play my tenth grade solo at the Spring Concert. I hadn't had a conversation with you for some time, because of church and my brothers and sisters. But at that moment, and all of the others through life, I communicated and learned how to love you and to be a man through your eyes. I love you dad, forever today, and forever tomorrow." Romelo kissed his father, and gently sat down in the corner. Winton II felt the warm tears leave his eyes, but never felt them on his face. With all of the emotions, he felt that it was time, and he prayed for the pain was unbearable. He waved to his wife, and she arose, knowing what time it was. The two stared at each other, as she choked back her tears.

"Love, I'm going to call the pastor." Winton II shook his head no, and in silence they sat, waiting for the Passover.

An hour passed, and the nurse at the front desk strolled to the rear to speak with the family. Francis Poitner, RN was her name.

"Wake up all, I think it's time. Your father and grandfather is no longer speaking and his vitals signs are low. He can still hear, and see, but life is fading quickly."

Her walkie-talkie goes off.

"What's that Allena? Oh, a pastor is here? Send him back."

And as the man strolled back, the room collectively exhaled. The one man who supported their father, who supported their mother, and at one point or another, supported them all, came into the room with a bible and a smile. It was Winton III, and everyone collectively grabbed hands and prayed. Winton III strolled into his father's crypt and immediately, Winton II vital signs perked up. Without words, he prays for his father, and his mother clutched his hand and his father's. In a span of three hours, he realized that his life was for the sacrifice of others, and not only would he live on through them, but they had lived through and will forever live through him. And as his soul reached for the Golden Thrown, his last word was Amen. Winton II passed over.

Reality Check:
Mr. and Mrs. Irrelevant

Dead to the World so it seems, staring at a dimming horizon while gently patting my belly. Hunger overwhelms me as acceptance escapes my reaches. I stare off unto the here nor there. What is it about America that I can never quite understand? Everything about me has been taken from a stanza of the inferno. Any happiness or functionality that I happen upon is due to the hard work that I inject into my presence. It's no secret that I hail from an Africa that no longer exists. A place where at one point, her and I, whoever she was, sat on the coast of white sand, and warm horizon with fire logs burning before us. Ember's sprinting towards the horizon as our naked bodies felt the World turning within us. Man and woman, uninhibited with such terms as justice and equality, for we were just in whatever we did freely, and equal in rights as human beings, but woman knowing her role, and man making sure that in performing her role she was happy. That was the time that we were slaves for the debt we owed or for the sweet potato seeds we needed to start our own fortunes. Somehow, shortly after the waning dusk, I lost her to a strange group of people. They tied and roped her; a few men had their way with her. I myself was roped and beaten, someone, maybe the soothsayer or clansmen told them I was a slave. They took me and introduced me to my hell and the people who would forever subject me to hell, as well as to the chains that I was to wear until the end of time. And she, well we would never see each other again how we saw each other that night. On that beach, tied and solid, I waved goodbye to my woman, waiting to endure what new definitions would be afforded to this man. All women that I loved would change. I had no idea what new woman I would find solace in. Years later, I'm beaten, left not to read, nor tell my history to neither her nor anyone. Someone whose hair looks like mine, and who soul feels like mine, and who laughs at my stories. Who are they to laugh?

I sit undisturbed for the moment, wondering how I now sit in a free place that I call America and home, and yet it feels like I am but a stranger. My mother and father, grandparents live here, their parents lived here, their parents' parents died here, yet I still remain a stranger to anyone around. I carry a host of chains; whether they are fashionable and by choice, or rusted unconscious chains that I was burdened with some time ago, I love these chains for some reason. Maybe it's the self-loathing and self-disrespect that I love so much. I knew the woman I once knew would not be the woman that I would need to know on this day that I am feeling so low. She has been brainwashed and doesn't trust me nor love me. She doesn't even give me a chance to be with her. Unless she can have the deception of anti-social behavior associated with me, I am neither of use nor am I worth the interest to her. I'm more like her hard working father, who speaks well, and is respectful, and who would remain humble in every small thing about her, including having the honor to hold her hand under a sky made for us. So I would encourage her to believe. More humble than the boy who stands on he corner selling false hopes to pheens, and the same thing to you, with the audacity to whistle for you to bring your ass on. To some women, that's life as they want it, and that which is peddled into their mind by the deceptions of their own neglect- their black men. Before, all that she needed from me was food, a fire, and my stern watch and steady hand. My smile and the deep horizons within my glare used to let her know that today is a new and positive day, and tonight we shall sleep to rest for our celebration of another day. America is the home of the brave and land of the free? What happened to the home of the desolate, home of the

brainwashed, home of our debtors, home of our
inflictors, and home of our chains, home of the
ignorant that willingly allow this thing; division,
to go on? I guess that means nothing. I have but
three to four hundred years experience here in this
new place and another couple of hundred in this
new culture which is devoid of my own, and I
continue to strive. Though I have chains that I
carry, and my history is sung and spoken over
music-one has to be of a special breed to interpret
its true meanings- I remain hopeful and optimistic
in a system that continuously rejects me. A mere
glimpse of my story's light words, or sweet
melody, or strum, blow, or whistle can never tell
you about me unless you ask.

So why is it that I and my woman have fought to
build this country, fought to fight its wars, fought
to pave its streets, design its buildings, tweak its
social brain, and still feel like our bellies are
screaming for more nourishment, from one
another and this place? It's hard to realize that
indeed, you have been and will be an expendable
commodity. Drug dealers, pimps, and even
womanizers implore the same tactics. Get a few of
your boys together, buy that pound, sell it, exploit
people, lose yourself, gain hell, hook people,

whistle to the women children of the people you exploit and make zombie-they use something or most importantly someone else to get what they need underneath the radar, and when the kingdom is built they toss them and have no use for them. All of this to receive favor with any of the latter, i.e., the dealt, pimped, and the womanized realize that they sort of enjoy the system they are stuck in, feeling like they deserve something for their enslavement. Slavery is what they begin to enjoy and find solace in. Anything good outside of slavery is in fact ludicrous. And it's not like the enslaved love their environments because of brutal tactics, but it's because its all one knows and appreciates it all for what it offers; security. She is no longer worried about the touch of him to quell her inner infidelities. There is a system to do that now. And like that, I likened myself to a modern day slave. Chains a'hangin', words meaning nothing because my soul left me long ago, while my woman attempts to pick up the slack, but can't do much, because what she's attracted to is of the diseased variety, mentally enslaved, socially enslaved, lost to a host of another's inferno's-black man. She remains across the bridge, and I stand on the other side waving for no apparent reason. She watches me, you can tell how each time I wave and call her lovely name, requesting her soul over a glass of wine and a book on love, and she smirks but can only see the deception that is in front of her. But apparently, one can only realize what has been forced fed into one's reality. She has known for some time; prosperity, delusion, infidelity, hypocrisy, injustice, inhumanity, fake love, only to truly not know real love when it pops in. Don't be mad at me be mad at the system. Regardless who you might vote for, what school you might go to, the white woman you might marry, the thug that you might fall in love with, you are of your own World, which continues to spin as it shall. And while the rest of the World and the truly free continue to grow, one should realize, that until we enlighten ourselves with introspection, devoid of the crap that American society tells you to play, the more and more you and I should address each other as Mr. And Mrs. Irrelevant. I arise from the night air and walk along the various routes back to anywhere, preparing myself to get blown, having to stroll pass people who have no intentions to even say hello in the first place, when they look and see the same struggle in my eyes as I see in theirs, my counterpart no less. We sign off as Mr. and Mrs. Irrelevant.

AFTERTHOUGHTS

I hope that I have encouraged some to venture out and think beyond the narrow passages and constricted corridors of society, vying for their inner-self instead. I hope that I have pierced a small hole through the dark tint of the weary blind. Please see the light of your own truths, even if that light gives only a glimpse of its beauty. I offer mental fire for the despondent scholar. To the creative writer, I offer a new reason to criticize. I sincerely implore your criticism to be of your own beliefs and actions. Not those planted and reaped in your mind by others (parents, family, peers, and society).

Without inner struggles, inner feelings, and inner issues, churned from courage and convictions, would we be classified as human beings? I have my own opinion for this question and many others. It doesn't matter what I think. If you're adventurous as I, you would sit down and dialogue with yourself about questions that consciously or unconsciously spark your imagination. Allow it to grab your un-divided attention. My personal afterthoughts are summed up as such; will writing such a thing affect the relationships that I have gained with people? Will what I love to do really bare reward as others say it would? Lastly, if I really cared about either of these aforementioned afterthoughts, would I truly be a mind unhinged? I hope that I will have the resources and the time to devote my undivided artistic attention to you all via creative writing, for it has become my blood, my oxygen and my deliverance from a World in which I am here nor there. Regardless of whatever circumstance, I will continue, line for line, for this piece was more or less an ode to what I've known, and what I want to break way from as a human being, but most importantly an artist. For a fictional piece, it was definitely a heavy spill to put on paper. Dependent upon the feedback from myself, I will continue to write in the same vain. Most likely, I will be on another level, in another place, with a new realm of ideas and perspective, coupled with the realities of the World that we all live in. Regardless of where I'll be on paper, you are always welcomed to indulge in the smaller things with me, and are more than welcomed to follow me. Where I'll be is neither here nor there.

With Peace and Blessings